MARINA MAN
A Southern California Novel
Of Crime and Confusion
By Jonathan Schwartz

From Magic Lamp Press
Venice, California

Magic Lamp
Press ™

www.MagicLampPress.com

This is a work of fiction. Any resemblance to actual persons, living or dead is entirely coincidental.

MARINA MAN
A Southern California Novel
Of Crime and Confusion

This book, may not be reproduced in any form, stored in a retrieval system, or transmitted by any means, electronic, mechanical, by photocopying, recording, or otherwise, without written permission from the publisher, Magic Lamp Press. For permission, contact: Editor Gene Grossman at Magic Lamp Press, P.O. Box 9547, Marina del Rey, CA 90295. or gene_grossman@yahoo.com
.....

The Tom McGuire Series
http://www.legalmystery.com

Cover photography ©MMVIII Greg Wenger
http://www.marinadelreyphotos.com/

ISBN: 1-882629-67-1

To Joan, who proved there was such a thing as love at first sight.

1

Maria and I caught a Mako shark about two miles off Malibu on Sunday morning. When we got back to Marina del Rey, a Sheriff's Department boat was waiting for us in the main channel. We were escorted to the Harbor Patrol dock, where we were arrested for shooting at whales. We stood on the dock in plastic handcuffs, in bright sunshine, while people stared at us as if we were standing in the dock at Nuremberg. We looked at each other. We were obviously sharing a ridiculous dream.

Young deputy Carmichael. Neat auburn moustache. Tight khaki over gymnasium-nurtured muscles. The type of Southern Californian with whom I sometimes have a language problem. His clear, sincere, judgmental gaze now fixed on Maria, angry and gorgeous in her tiny yellow bikini, tan skin, straw hat. I urge evidence of shark carcass with bullet holes. There it is, hanging on the transom of our boat; maybe six feet long, probably a little over a hundred and twenty-five pounds. Obviously not a whale. The argument backfires; the shark is proof we were out in the Bay shooting. A whale would not fit in our sixteen-foot runabout. Logic.

Deputy Carmichael squints at us: you think I'm stupid? He's going to keep custody of Maria's perfectly good Smith & Wesson .357 Magnum with five-inch barrel. For this she gives me an evil look; my fault? Carmichael thinks the shark might be evidence; wants to hang on to it, but where? Some discussion almost out of earshot; County Coroner has either refused to allow the shark in his morgue, or they're afraid to ask for fear of ridicule. It is not illegal to catch sharks. Shark is hauled up on the dock, measured, photographed, three bullet holes counted.

A photographer from the *L.A. Times* took our picture, then shark pictures. Deputy Carmichael took off my handcuffs and we hauled the Mako into my boat and covered it with a tarp, to protect it from the sun. Then they took us to jail.

Apparently, a woman on the porch of a beachfront house in Malibu had been watching us with binoculars while we were lining in the shark. At that point, just before I gaffed it and Maria roped it up, Maria shot the shark. This is fairly standard practice for shark fishermen. I don't think you can kill a shark by shooting it with a gun, at least not right away, but it does slow them down, and that makes things a little safer while the shark is at arm's length. A shot shark will not qualify for an International Game Fish Association line class record, but I think it's better to end a day's fishing with the same number of body parts you had when you started.

The woman with the binoculars couldn't see the shark, since it was under water, and when she heard the gunfire she decided we were shooting at whales. Never mind that the whales would have been under water too. If there had been any whales. I was told she was the wife of a Los Angeles County Assistant Prosecutor, which may explain why she picked up the phone and reported us to the Harbor Patrol in Marina del Rey. I wondered how an Assistant Prosecutor could afford a beachfront house in Malibu.

My bail bondsman giggled when I told him what the problem was, but he had us back on the street in four hours. We were due to be arraigned in Santa Monica Municipal Court in two weeks. We were able to recover the Mako shark and take it back to my dock, where I dressed it out. It fed everyone on the dock that night. I marinated the steaks in a mixture of soy sauce and sesame oil, and barbecued them for about seven minutes on a side. I felt like the Little Red Hen; everyone wants to help you eat the shark, but nobody will volunteer to do your time.

The next day was Monday, and I got up late. Maria had gone back to her family's home in San Gabriel the night before, on her Harley. I sat and drank coffee on board *Den Mother*, the forty-eight foot post-war Chris-Craft powerboat that was my home, reflecting on our new incarnation as ecological criminals. The *LA Times* delivery person brought the paper out to the end of the dock and left it on my dock step. We had made the city page:

BOATERS ARRESTED IN MARINA DEL REY

Marina attorney Thomas McGuire and LA County employee Maria Zaragoza were arrested in Marina del Rey Sunday after a witness reported seeing the pair shooting at whales from a small boat in Santa Monica Bay...

No pictures. Would the D.A. reject this? Would it matter that we had come back in with a shark carcass with bullet holes in it? I reflected on the fact that the actual evidence, such as it was, had been eaten. What would a Santa Monica jury do to us? People loved whales these days and would probably deal harshly with anyone accused of doing anything to hurt them.

Everyone I met that day had seen the story. The other lawyers in the suite thought it was hilarious. They called me 'Ahab.' Lawyers; tell them you got arrested and they laugh. It was nothing new. My fishing activities had earned me the nickname 'Sharky.' My part-time efforts at standup comedy

9

were known. The consensus was that I was strange; not like the other ducklings. I was the East Coast, Ivy League bust-out who had gone from a job at the U.S. Attorney's Office downtown to a Marina del Rey practice and a home on a classic mahogany Chris-Craft in 'C' Basin.

What could they do to us? A fine? Probation? Maria worked for the County, and could be fired if she was convicted of a crime. Nobody could fire me; I'm self-employed.

*   *   *

Murray Markoff called the office, but it wasn't to kid me about my weekend exploits. "I'll buy you sushi," he said. "I've got a little *tsurris.*"

I've never liked sushi, but the people who do like it tend to nag you to death if you don't join them. I've found it's easier to eat it then to argue about it. Murray was retired from a career that involved horse racing and gambling somewhere in New York. He was a little man with a fringe of white hair on a tanned bald head. He looked like somebody's kindly old grandfather until he opened his mouth. Then he sounded like a character out of *Guys and Dolls*; a kindly old retired bookie. These days Murray mostly drew his Social Security and worked on his tan. He lived in the Marina on a boat called *Gefilte Fish.*

Murray's Yiddish accent reminded me of my childhood in the Bronx. My mother had taught me some Yiddish. The only unJewish thing anyone had ever heard of her doing, evidently, was to choose a New York Irish labor lawyer to marry. There was shock and horror on both sides of the proposed union. Multiculturalism was not fashionable in the Bronx at that time, at least not among the Irish or the Jews. I was a little boy with sandy hair, freckles and an Irish name, who spoke a little Yiddish. It led to some strange moments.

When I worked as a musician in the Catskills between college years, the MC would pick on me on slow nights. "Look at the drummer," he would say to an audience of middle-class Jewish businessmen and their wives, "the only goy in the whole hotel." Big laugh. Then I would say *"kish mir in tuchis."* Kiss my ass. Bigger laugh. I think that was when I decided I'd rather be the comedian than the drummer. So, whenever I could I'd get them to put me in the Thursday night show; amateur night. It was scary enough being up there; I didn't take chances with my material. I would insult the guests:

SO, A GUEST CALLS THE FRONT DESK AND SAYS
"HEY, I GOTTA LEAK IN MY BATHTUB."
THE CLERK SAYS "GO AHEAD."

Or the entertainment:

THE BAND WAS SO BAD HERE LAST SEASON THAT
SOMEONE STARTED UP A TRUCK IN THE PARKING LOT
AND TWO COUPLES GOT UP TO DANCE.

Or I would go with my Irish-Jewish background and mine the culture clash:

MY FATHER'S CATHOLIC AND MY MOTHER'S JEWISH. I GO
TO CONFESSION, BUT I BRING MY LAWYER.

I stole all the material, of course. It was old when I stole it, and it wasn't that funny to begin with. Back home in the Bronx I had Lenny Bruce records I would play by the hour. I had a few of his routines down pat, but his nervous energy eluded me. Maybe it would have been easier if I had grown up in a burlesque house and been a drug addict, like Lenny. All my life I've had to get by without these early advantages.

In those Catskills amateur shows I was playing it safe; the curse of a beginner. Later I learned you can't be safe and funny. But back then it was being up there that counted; standing on a stage with a microphone in my hand. Ready to die if they didn't like me. But getting laughs, when I got

11

them, was an indescribable thrill. I had been warned about drug addiction but nobody warned me about standup.

*   *   *

Murray worked part time for the Southern California Sea Pioneers, a charitable organization based in Marina del Rey, which claimed to provide boating and fishing activities for inner city kids. In fact, what they did was to accept charitable donations of used boats at inflated values, then sell the boats for cash, sometimes paying kickbacks to the people who donated the boats in the first place. Murray was the bagman; he made the payoffs. Apart from these activities, it was questionable what, if anything, the Sea Pioneers actually did. Murray claims he's never seen a young person on the premises. He refers to the organization as the Southern California Sea Snakes.

I sat next to Murray at the sushi bar and tried to select something recognizable from the photographs on the menu. Sushi or no sushi, I was glad to be out of the office. I had spent an intense morning with a new client, a bearded sculptor who had been charged with several felonies for shot-gunning a four-story-high outdoor sculpture attached to a building not far from the beach. His target was a huge mechanized representation of a dancing ballerina with a clown mask over her face; a work of breathtaking ugliness which had nevertheless been lavishly praised by the LA art establishment. My client said most public art was 'plaza plop,' and wanted me to base his defense on the idea that, by attempting to destroy this monstrosity, he had been doing everyone a favor. He was also worried that the police might not give him back his shotgun. In addition to the beard, he had wild eyes; a crazed look. It made a bad image when you imagined him with the shotgun. I didn't give much for his chances in court, but, hey, a solo law practice can be a bit of a circus. You take what you get and do what you can with it.

So I ordered some damn sushi and while we waited I asked Murray what was on his mind. He looked over his

12

shoulder as if he was still working Flatbush Avenue, booking bets and dodging vice heat. But there was only the sushi chef behind the counter, knife flashing. Murray was wearing a new addition to his large collection of aloha shirts, along with the usual faded jeans and boat shoes.

"I think one of my best deals is going south on me," he said. "You remember the sixty-three foot Pacemaker?"

I remembered it. When I last saw this aging wooden powerboat, it had been abandoned at the local boatyard, where they were trying to sell it for some $3,000 in uncollected dock fees. Its owner had done some sort of insurance scam, gotten a settlement and walked, after stripping the boat of everything he could carry. I had gone aboard out of curiosity. You don't find many sixty-three foot twin-diesel powerboats selling for $3,000. It was sad. The boat was a mess, thoroughly vandalized. It stank below decks of dry rot. All of her navigational electronics were gone. Pigeons were nesting in the control bridge, their droppings and nesting materials adding to the general sense that this was a vessel that would go to sea no more. But she did have a pair of huge diesel engines and the hull looked OK from a distance. I figured some fool would be suckered into buying her sooner or later. After a few months, she disappeared from her slip at the boat yard and I figured I had been right about the fool, but apparently Murray had been involved somehow.

"Murray," I said, "hold the phone. Are you trying to tell me that somebody donated the Pacemaker to the Sea Pioneers?"

"It was my most beautiful deal. Just paper, no boat."

"Sure there was a boat," I said. "I was on board"

"It was too big, Tommy. Too big and too old. So good-bye boat. Who needed it? The only thing is, the doctor got a letter from the Government about it. Hersh is shitting blue butter beans. He wants to fire me."

Hersh I knew; he was the Director of the Sea Pioneers.

"Who's the doctor?"

"Doctor Rayburn. He's a proctologist in Santa Monica. I was his patient last year and we got to talking. I told him about the Sea Pioneers, but he said he didn't have a boat to donate. So I thought of the Pacemaker. Nobody else wanted it. Now I think maybe I made a mistake and got everyone in trouble. The Doctor is really mad at me. Could you go over and talk to him?" He nibbled halfheartedly on a piece of giant clam.

"Help me out here," I said. "The Doctor donates the boat to the Sea Pioneers, and gets to deduct its value on his taxes, right?"

"Right."

"But Murray, the boat wasn't worth anything."

"Ah ha!" He waved a chopstick in the air.

"Oh... ok. How did you do it?"

Murray laughed, spraying small fragments of what looked like pickled ginger and rice onto his shirt's garish pattern of palm trees and hula dancers.

"That's the beauty part. When I was on board I found a survey they did ten years ago when she was in good shape. It said the boat was worth three hundred thousand. All I had to do was copy it and change the date. Hersh has it in the file. I never thought we'd have to show it to anyone. I explained it to Doctor Rayburn after he got the letter and he was bouncing off the chandelier. He said he was going to kill me."

"That's what he said?"

"Actually, he said he'd kill me if he got audited."

14

2

The next morning I called Doctor Rayburn's office from the boat and got an eleven-thirty appointment. I drove up Lincoln Boulevard from the Marina and east on Santa Monica Boulevard to somewhere around 22nd street in Santa Monica, where doctors congregate like schools of anchovies. I sat in Doctor Rayburn's waiting room eyeing photographs of big-breasted, third-world maidens in a two-year-old National Geographic and wondering whether a little proctology humor would be misunderstood. All I could remember was the one about how a proctoscope was a long tube with an asshole at either end. Probably not a good choice. Before I could think of another one, I was walking into Doctor Rayburn's office.

Central Casting could not have done Doctor Rayburn better than he did himself. He was wearing the first three-piece black and white herringbone tweed suit I had seen since law school. Every part of him, his hair, his clothing, his features, looked polished and then coated with a good grade of spray lacquer. He looked a lot like a statue. He seemed to shine and I had the thought that having achieved this remarkable degree of perfection, he should now be perma-plaqued and hung on the wall of his own office. Doctor Rayburn was a monument to himself. Suddenly, it spoke.

"You are associated with Mr. Markoff, I believe."

Only his eyes suggested that he was inhabited by a human being. They looked bewildered; the eyes of a lost puppy.

"He's a friend of mine," I said. "I'm a lawyer and sometimes I handle legal work for him."

"Do you by chance also represent the Southern California Sea Pioneers?"

"No, Doctor Rayburn, I don't."

"Your friend has given me some very bad advice, very bad. I have tax trouble now because of him and his Pioneers."

I glanced around his office. It was lavishly over-furnished in a style his decorator had probably described as Louis Quatorze. My father would have called it Whorehouse Revival. On a wall, in addition to the usual diplomas and certificates, were dozens of photographs of Doctor Rayburn hanging out with actors, politicians and sports figures. Some fancy fannies had lingered hereabouts.

"Help me understand this, Doctor. Mr. Markoff was your patient, right?"

"Yes, you are correct. Multiple hemorrhoidectomy, no complications." So much for patient confidentiality.

"And isn't it fair to say that he's a little old guy with practically no hair who talks like a Damon Runyon character and wears Hawaiian shirts and blue jeans?"

"I suppose you could say that."

"Doctor, did Mister Markoff ever tell you anything about his education or any professional qualifications that he might have?"

"Never. Nothing."

It was time to roll my eyes. I rolled them.

17

"And you say you took tax advice from this guy?"

Snap goes the trap. Rayburn was not used to being tweaked. He blinked at me and gave me his best 'I'm the doctor' look.

"What is it you want with me, Mister McGuire?"

"Look, Doctor, you're an educated man." A dubious proposition, but I figured he'd go for it. "Your deal with Murray was baloney, as you know. You bought a tax dodge and it blew up. Murray has a lot of friends in the marina. I'm one of them. I think you should pay the Government what it wants and hope nobody figures out what happened. That way, you won't get in any worse trouble than you're in already. If you try to put Murray on the spot, he may decide he'd be better off as a Government witness. The U.S. Attorney's Office loves to prosecute doctors. I know, I used to work there."

I wasn't sure how much of this free legal advice Doctor Rayburn had taken in. The puzzled puppy was still looking out from inside the statue. The interview was over.

"I have surgery, Mr. McGuire, if you will excuse me."

As I turned to go I took a last look at Doctor Rayburn's ego wall. One photograph depicted Doctor R. seated at a restaurant table with two men who did not appear to be actors, politicians or sports figures. Suddenly I was looking at some familiar faces; a couple of middle-aged boys who were big but not beautiful. Together they represented most of the middle management of a major Southern California organized crime family. We used to study their pictures on a big chart when I worked at the Federal Building. Proctologist to the stars I could believe, but proctologist to the Mob?

"So long Doctor R," I said. "If my bum goes on the fritz, I'll be back."

He looked at me blankly. Sometimes you just gotta throw them away.

When I got back to the boat, there were two messages on my answering machine: *'Beep'* "This is Harry Hatcher with the *Los Angeles Times*. We're doing another story about whales. Call me back if you'd like to make a statement for publication." He left a telephone number that I did not write down. Then *'Beep,'* followed by a long hesitation. You could tell somebody was out there, and finally the sound of a hang-up. This sort of thing always gives me the creeps. It's like receiving a communication from the dead. I once read a book about experiences of people who claimed they had received phone calls from deceased friends or relatives. I don't think it's impossible. I get phone calls from people I wish were dead. Is there such a big difference?

3

It's hard to explain living aboard to those who haven't had the pleasure. Most people's initial impulse is to assume that you lack essential comforts that everyone else enjoys. You get asked questions like "How do you cook," or by the more outspoken, "Where does it go when you flush?"

Actually, a large well-designed powerboat can offer living conditions approaching luxury with privacy to a degree usually unattainable on land at any price. Like all powerboats, *Den Mother* is full of machines and electrical systems of all kinds, and successful living aboard requires some degree of understanding of them, if not complete mastery. Living aboard is walking from your car to your boat with two bottles of Bordeaux in one hand and a battery charger in the other.

I parked and walked to the gangway of my dock. It was five o'clock in the afternoon. It was bright. It was Monday. The temperature was somewhere comfortably in the low seventies and I remembered Neil Simon's joke: 'When it's a hundred and five degrees in New York, it's seventy-two in Los Angeles. When it's five below zero in New York, it's seventy-two in Los Angeles. There are at least two hundred and fifty thousand interesting people in New York, and seventy-two in Los Angeles.' The lingering snobbery of an East Coast émigré. I'll cop to it.

I put the sculptor and his shotgun out of my mind. I was home. I could tell because there was Bobby Baxter, still putting away trolling gear after his weekend of marlin fishing. His thirty-six foot Egg Harbor sport fisher was the finest at the dock, and it was Baxter's mission in life to keep it that way. It was rumored that he had a wife and children, but Bobby and his boat *Bobby's Egg* was all we ever saw.

"Bobby," I said, "Did you kill any fish?"

Something had obviously not gone right for Bobby. His normally tan face assumed a rich reddish-purple hue. Captain, his little Maltese Terrier, looked up at us apprehensively. Bobby waived a big Rapala articulated minnow at me as he spoke:

"You're not gonna believe it. We ran all night and were off San Miguel Island at four. We were drifting and setting up to troll when this searchlight was suddenly shining at us and some dork with a loud hailer was shouting he was the Coast Guard and had two fifty-caliber machine guns pointed at us. Then there were rubber rafts full of Coasties with guns and we got boarded and searched. They were looking for drugs, I guess, but all they could find was my Dramamine and some beer. We were supposed to be trolling at dawn. By the time they left it was about eight o'clock and dawn was over and we were too pissed off to fish. So we drank our beer, ate our lunch and came back. You're a lawyer, Sharky, what do you say. Can I sue?"

"Sure you can. Anyone with a typewriter and a filing fee can sue. Who would you like to sue?"

"Whaddaya mean, 'who'? The Coast Guard, of course. Who're we talking about?"

Most boaters don't realize the Coast Guard can stop

and search your boat whenever, on a whim, or if they don't like your tie. Most Americans have the reasonable idea that your boat, which can easily cost more than a house, is your castle, and they think something is wrong when a crowd of machine-gun toting yahoos in uniform suddenly appear on board without asking permission. I figured it was useless to explain this to Bobby. Give the public what it wants.

"OK, we'll do it," I said, "and after the Court throws our case out the Coast Guard will put you and your boat on a permanent shit list. Maybe they'll put me on too. It'll be sort of like a curse. They'll be boarding and searching *Bobby's Egg* years from now when you and I are history."

Bobby turned and gave his beautiful sport fisher a nervous look. I think it worried him to imagine the boat without him around to take care of it. Actually, I felt the same way about *Den Mother*. The funny thing about Bobby and his twin diesel fishing machine was that the boat was in much better shape than Bobby, who was at least thirty pounds overweight and began each weekend at the dock with a can of Spar varnish and a quart of Johnny Walker Black Label. I sometimes wondered whether he drank the varnish or the scotch, but by Sunday afternoon both were usually gone.

*   *   *

In my galley, there was a stainless steel bucket full of fresh shrimp and ice. Maria had been to the Santa Monica street market that morning and I had two pounds of ridgebacks to clean. They had been caught off Santa Barbara the day before. They are not like ordinary shrimp. Each ridgeback is like a tiny Tyrannosaurus Rex, imbedded in a thick, spiny shell that tends to injure you when you pick it up. If ridgebacks were war materiel, they would be tanks. They taste better than lobster. To clean them it is first necessary to have a drink.

From the seawall I heard the deep, obnoxious roar of a Harley Davidson. Maria had arrived. Today, at least, the roar wasn't getting any closer. When we first got to know each other, Maria had the habit of riding her Harley down the gangway and out onto the dock. True, there was no rule that you couldn't ride motorcycles on the dock, but the Dockmaster had objected to it. It also frightened the ducks.

Maria was the beautiful early-thirties daughter of a large Mexican-American family in the San Gabriel Valley. She had brothers with homemade tattoos, who may or may not have been members of street gangs. Maria worked for the L.A. County Department of Adult Protective Services, and was often involved in disputes between elderly unwanted parents and children who found it necessary to either abandon or cannibalize the old folks in one way or another. Maria favored handguns for the elderly, and suggested that they be used liberally when grown children settle on the assets of their aging parents like locusts on a beet field.

When I looked up again, she was standing on the dock outside the salon hatch and smiling at me.

"*Ola, mi carino*," she said.

Maria could sound poetic when she spoke her native language, but I had been suspicious of her little Spanish phrases ever since a date I had with her many years ago, when Los Angeles was new enough to me to make a meal in a Mexican restaurant seem exotic. When we had finished eating I asked her to teach me the Spanish for 'where is the men's room,' and she taught me a phrase that turned out to mean 'fuck your grandmother,' which caused a riot when I tried it out on the waiter.

Maria put her hair up to go to work, and wore a conservative blue suit and pumps. It made an interesting contrast to her dark, Hispanic good looks. To ride the Harley to and from work she would take off the pumps and wear cute little motorcycle boots. I doubt that anyone at the County Department of Adult Protective Services knew that she kept a .357 Magnum in a compartment on the Harley. Loaded. "It's useless unless it's loaded," she would say. The gun had been hard for me to get used to. My mother was Jewish. When I was growing up the most dangerous thing in our home was an electric carving knife. This had its funny side:

JEWS DON'T RELATE TO GUNS BECAUSE GUNS DON'T SOUND JEWISH. YOU KNOW; COLT, WINCHESTER, REMINGTON. NOW, IF JEWS COULD BUY A 45 CALIBER SCHWARTZ & WEISSBERG, OR A 30.06 SEMIAUTOMATIC FINKELSTEIN...

You don't get many gun owners in comedy club audiences, so the laughs are there.

I PICKED OUT A HANDGUN AND PAID FOR IT, AND THE SALESMAN SAID THERE WAS A TWO-WEEK WAITING PERIOD BEFORE I COULD TAKE IT HOME. THAT'S STUPID. HOW DID HE EXPECT ME TO STAY DRUNK AND ANGRY FOR TWO WEEKS?

*   *   *

After coming on board Maria had immediately let her hair down, changed into shorts and a tee, and removed her shoes. They wouldn't have recognized her downtown. She stood in the galley, putting away her purchases and getting ready to cook for us. She looked tropical, her skin a toasty golden color. She had a body that could, and did, stop traffic. Once, when she had taken the Harley over to the other side of the Marina to run an errand, in sandals and wearing her yellow Bikini, she told me she had seen a major intersection collision between two drivers who couldn't take their eyes off the dark-haired toasty-golden girl in the little yellow bathing suit riding the big black Harley. Or so she said, with some satisfaction. I looked down into the galley and thought how lucky I was to have her, how exotic she would always be to me. I imagined her naked, in a grass hut on the Yucatan, under a jim-jam tree. Remember, I grew up in the Bronx.

I went down to the galley, stealthily crept up behind her as she stood at the stove, and took off her shorts. It's one of the advantages of a home without children.

Maria said "I'm trying to cook dinner."

25

I said "Just relax. You don't have to stop what you're doing."

And she didn't, almost.

Later, we ate the ridgebacks, popovers and a salad, and watched the news on TV. There was a story about an attempted carjacking and murder that afternoon on Mindanao Way in the Marina. Even on the small screen you could see it was a large gold Mercedes sedan with the personal plate *DERRIER*. Damned if Doctor Rayburn hadn't been shotgunned for his car right down the street from us. The perpetrator had not been apprehended. The victim was taken from the scene by ambulance and pronounced dead at the V.A. Hospital in Westwood. I guessed that Doctor Rayburn hadn't been wearing the black and white herringbone tweed suit. It had certainly looked bulletproof to me.

Images flickered before us of blown out glass, uniforms and barricades, then anchor-people, clucking remorse: 'What is the city coming to?' I ate more ridgebacks. The trick is that after you shuck them out of their shells you put them in boiling water for no more than a minute or ninety seconds, then put them under cold running water to stop the cooking process. All cookbooks tell you to leave them in for three minutes or more. It's very bad advice. Boil a shrimp for three minutes and you can use it to drive a nail. I'd enjoy ridgebacks better if they weren't so hard to clean.

I told Maria about my meeting with Doctor Rayburn, the unexpected faces on his ego wall and his troubles with the Government. It was upsetting to me; I had just met with the poor guy that morning, now he gets killed on the street a few blocks from my dock.

Maria said "Why don't you call Larry Hayden and ask him if he knows anything about this?"

Larry had worked with me at the U.S. Attorney's Office in downtown L.A. The life had suited Larry better than it did me, and he was still there, now risen to the rank of Branch Chief. It made him sound like a bird. I got him at home on the first ring.

"Larry, how is everything at the Government?"

"Is this McGuire? Sorry to hear about your whale problem."

This could have been a decent set-up but it's not possible to kid a federal civil servant. There is something incurably unfunny about their lives. A damp spot that can't be dried.   Maria sat across the galley table in the semi-darkness and listened as I spoke.

"Larry, how about Doctor Rayburn on the tube tonight?"

"Yeah, somebody was hitchhiking the hard way."

Larry Hayden, master of the snappy comeback.

I remembered the photograph in Doctor Rayburn's office and made a guess: "You know Doctor Rayburn was connected. What's the story?"

There was a pause. Larry was thinking whether he still trusted me enough to gossip with me about his work.

"Sharky, that's your nickname now, huh?"

He had decided I was not going to hear whatever little nuggets he had.

"Come on Larry, don't be mean to me. This is Tommy talkin' to ya." There's nothing like an Al Jolson impression when you really need one.

"Oh, I hate it when you beg. Ok. We think Doctor Rayburn did plastic surgery for certain persons who didn't want to be recognized. He had some training but he's not board-certified and I don't think they liked the results. The last guy he did, we got him on a phone tap saying his face turned out looking like it fell off in the street and got run over by a truck. We don't know what he looked like after the doctor got through with him. A contract killer named Joe Zito, from Boston. Look, McGuire…" I could feel something coming I wasn't going to like. "…I had to send a memo back to Washington about the whales. We've got animal rights types in the Department, just like in L.A. Those are Federally protected marine mammals, man. Didn't you ever hear the slogan 'save the whales'?"

27

I had done a piece of stage business on this:

PEOPLE WHO SAY 'SAVE THE WHALES?'
WHAT IF YOU COULD SAVE THE WHALES? WHERE WOULD
YOU PUT THEM?
WHAT DOES THIS BUMPERSTICKER MEAN –
'I LOVE WHALES?' SOUNDS GREAT, BUT HOW'RE YOU GOING
TO BRING IT OFF? THERE AREN'T GOING TO BE ANY
OPPORTUNITIES FOR INTIMACY.
AND THE PEOPLE WHO SAY THEY LOVE THEM, SOMETIMES
THEY GO OUT ON BOATS TO WATCH THE WHALES BREED.
THIS IS LOVE? HOW WOULD YOU LIKE TO BE MAKING LOVE
AND YOU LOOK UP AND YOUR BEDROOM'S FULL OF WHALES
– WATCHING YOU?
SO YOUR BUMPERSTICKER SHOULD READ 'I LOVE HAVING A
GOOD OPINION OF MYSELF –
'LOOK, IF YOU LOVE WHALES SO MUCH, SHOULDN'T YOU
LEAVE THEM ALONE? GIVE THEM A LITTLE PRIVACY?
IT'S ALL BULLSHIT – YOU KNOW WHAT YOUR
BUMPERSTICKER SHOULD READ?
'I ENJOY FEELING MORALLY SUPERIOR WHILE I AM EATING,
DRINKING, SMOKING, SHREDDING AND SCREWING
EVERYTHING I CAN GET MY GREEDY LITTLE HANDS ON.'
PUT THAT ON YOUR BIG FAT SUV.
DO YOU LIKE THAT?.... DO YOU LIKE THAT?

It was a rant. It wasn't particularly funny but I was screaming at them and they liked me for it, for the commitment. On the video I was mugging, making faces I had never seen before. Soaking wet. Took me days to come down. Maybe it isn't better than sex, but it's up there.

"Suppose I did save the whales, Larry, where would I put them?"

No reaction. Sometimes you just gotta throw them away.

*   *   *

As we cleaned up I considered the further comedic possibilities of the whales. I had difficulty taking the accusation of shooting whales seriously, even though experience has taught me this is a dangerous attitude to take toward a legal problem, especially your own legal problem. Nobody, you imagine, could possibly take something that stupid seriously. This can be a dangerous mistake; it is exactly the most self-evidently absurd proposition that can capture the Judge's attention. A lawyer should always remember; there is nothing so dumb that you can count on the Judge agreeing with you that it's dumb. It's almost as if Judges feel sorry for dumb ideas, like some people feel sorry for dumb animals. The Judge may want to help the poor dumb idea, like he would help an old blind beggar cross the street, or a lost dog, or an old blind prosecutor trying to convict Maria and me for shooting whales. Still, the hilarity of it kept calling to me; if only it had happened to someone else.

In the literature of standup comedy you can find a personality profile of the kind of person who becomes a comedian. It starts with a distant parent, like my father, stingy with praise. If I'm funny, the kid thinks, he'll like me. My mother says I was making jokes at two and a half. From this it's a short step to becoming the class clown, and from there it isn't long before you can find yourself with a microphone in your hand, facing a crowd of bored, drunken strangers. You've arrived.

Why comedy? Clearly, it was exposure to the Catskill Mountains during my formative years. When I started, I was seventeen. I thought I had died and gone to Heaven, up there on the bandstand every night in my tuxedo, reading charts for name acts, working alongside grown men supporting families, getting union scale. And, as it turned out, listening to comedians, many, many comedians, week after week; Henny Youngman, Rodney Dangerfield, Buddy Hackett; everyone working during that period of time who wasn't too dirty for a middle-class Jewish crowd. We played half-hours on and off for dancing, alternating with a Latin band, and we

29

rehearsed and played seven shows a week. Sunday nights there was a jam session at the River Tavern. We would come back to the hotel at dawn. Never since then have I felt so astoundingly hip; returning in the gray early morning, our hotel and its staff and guests fast asleep, after working out with the best jazz players from hotel bands all over the Catskills. Paralyzingly, world-class hip. It may all have been too much for what followed; college, law school, and life among the necktie-and-wingtip set

Somewhere along the way I picked up the idea that I would not operate down the middle, but around the edges. Then I went into one of the most down-the-middle professions there is. Go figure.

4

Mrs. Hilliard was very old. She sat in the Dockmaster's office, her aluminum walker in front of her. She wore a tailored tweed suit that had been expensive long ago, and good jewelry. She was making an effort to be alert, but I thought she looked dazed, apprehensive. Her wispy white hair needed a comb. It was just a few months after I had bought the boat, and I had stopped off at the Marina office to get my mail. The Dockmaster, Ms. Eckstrom, wanted me to talk to Mrs. Hilliard about problems she was having with her family.

A few minutes with the two ladies revealed that Mrs. Hilliard's husband had died the year before. Her children had put most of the contents of the home in storage, and moved her into a garden apartment at Leeward Marina. Also a form of storage, I thought. Her house had tenants in it now, but the rent didn't come to her. Alone in an unfamiliar setting, in a sparsely furnished apartment, marginally able to take care of herself, Mrs. Hilliard had serious difficulties managing her daily life. The bedroom was upstairs, the staircase steep. Not practical for an old person with two bad hips. And, Mrs. Hilliard told me, her children were now busy plundering her husband's estate. She missed her husband, missed her home and possessions, and whenever she could persuade a friend to drive her to her storage locker, more things would turn up missing. Her husband had evidently been quite a collector; coins, stamps, paintings, fine furniture, china. When she complained to her children they laughed at her. The missing objects had never existed, they said, or they had been sold by Mrs. Hilliard herself after her husband died, or Pop had sold them or given them away. Take your pick. Mrs. Hilliard cried as she described her plight. I looked over at Ms. Eckstrom. She was crying too. I felt like crying myself, but I'm a lawyer and we never cry.

I had some idea how to deal with the problems of abused old people, and when I got into the office later that day I called the L.A. County Department of Adult Protective Services and had a conversation with a supervisor. Was Mrs. Hilliard telling the truth? Were they stealing from her? She probably needed to be in a nursing home, before the day came when she fell down the stairs in her little garden apartment and solved her problems the hard way. And, we agreed, it was possible that she could afford better care, or it was possible that her family would have to be encouraged to accept their responsibilities to her. The case needed investigation. It was assumed that I would continue to be involved. By default, I had become Mrs. Hilliard's lawyer. A home visit was scheduled.

My client's apartment turned out to be half empty, and the things that were there had obviously come from someplace else, someplace much larger. I had never thought about it, but as living spaces tended to get smaller, furniture had become down-sized to fit the spaces. You don't necessarily notice things like this until you see what an old-fashioned horsehair, biscuit-tufted caramel leather sofa and two matching club chairs look like in a trendy little rental in

Marina del Rey. Think Hindenberg. Think Macy's Thanks-giving Day Parade. We are becoming a nation of dwarfs huddled in chicken coops full of doll furniture.

Mrs. Hilliard sat, thoroughly engulfed in one leather chair. I sat in the other. The County had sent us Ms. Zaragoza. She stood and asked questions in a businesslike little blue suit, black pumps. No jewelry. No wedding ring. Black hair up in what I later learned was called a French braid. I thought she might have been twenty-five; maybe five foot five, and compact. Light olive skin. A serious look. A little too much lipstick for my taste. Mostly she ignored me, but in a neutral way, nothing snotty. She made notes on a pad. I sat and tried to look helpful. Tried not to stare at her. Honestly, in that moment all I could think about was sex. I know what this sounds like, but I couldn't help it. I'm not going to lie to you.

Finally it was decided; we would visit the storage locker. Among other things, Mrs. Hilliard said there were papers in storage, including her husband's will and the inventory of his estate, other financial documents. The three of us drove there in Ms. Zaragoza's plain-vanilla motor pool white sedan, with the seal of L.A. County on the driver's door.

The self-storage place turned out to be a barracks-like affair; long stale-smelling corridors with locker doors stretching into the darkening distance. It was slow going for Mrs. Hilliard and her walker, but Ms. Zaragoza had apparently had plenty of practice; sauntering along beside us, keeping up a pleasant conversation with the old lady. We turned a corner and Mrs. Hilliard gasped, then stopped. "Oh," she said, "he's here."

Up ahead we could see an open locker door, and hear the sounds of someone moving things around inside. My client was plainly terrified of a confrontation, so we decided I would take her back to the car and Ms. Zaragoza would go on ahead. So Mrs. Hilliard and I slowly returned to the bleak parking area, where we waited in Ms. Zaragoza's County car, surrounded by parked RVs, boats on trailers, and a litter of what looked like building materials.

After a few minutes I heard shouting, and then a balding overweight man in his fifties exited the storage building at a dead run, pursued closely by Ms. Zaragoza, who was doing most of the shouting. I don't understand much Spanish, but she was plainly cursing at him. He had just enough lead time to jump into the front seat of a new-looking white Oldsmobile and lock the doors. His pursuer stood next to the car, panting. At that point Mrs. Hilliard's son (if that was who he was) should have started up the car and driven away. But he didn't. Instead, he made a mistake. He sat there and sneered at his pursuer, then gave her the finger. Ms. Zaragoza looked around, then stepped back and picked up a length of plumber's pipe off the tarmac and swung it against the car like you'd swing a baseball bat, smashing the driver's side window. The man inside recoiled with horror. So did I. I wasn't looking at Mrs. Hilliard, but I thought I heard her clapping her hands. Then the Oldsmobile started to move, burning rubber on the turns as it negotiated the parking lot. Ms. Zaragoza stood there breathing hard, still holding the piece of pipe.

At that moment I fell in love.

He had been drunk, she said, or at least lubricated enough to make a pass at her.

"He groped me," she said as she drove us back to the Marina. "That fat *pendejo* actually grabbed my behind."

I had never seen a woman like this. I didn't dare say a word.

After a minute she said, "Do you think he'll report it?" She looked over her shoulder at me in the backseat.

"You mean make a crime report?"

"Yeah. He could sue the County, too." But she smiled a little as she said it. There was a sense that maybe she would lose her job, but that it would have been worth it to see the slimeball's panic-stricken reaction as his window exploded all over him. I found myself hoping he had pissed his pants.

"Well," I said, "I don't see how he's going to make it stick. I saw him assault you."

She turned her head a little further around this time, and I felt like telling her to keep her eyes on the road. A look passed between us. Oh my God, I remember thinking, I've got a chance with this woman.

Then Mrs. Hilliard said "Don't you worry, honey." This was the first we had heard from her since the spectacular events in the parking lot. "That was my husband's car the little shit was driving. I wondered where it was. Mrs. Eckstrom and I reported it stolen."

5

As I walked into my office the next morning our receptionist Cathy was on the phone and made the gesture that means 'it's for you' with her hand over the receiver. She said Detective Radovich was on the line. Could that be right?

"Tell him I'm not here," I said. It sounded like a Doctor Rayburn-related call and I wanted to talk with Murray first.

"But you *are* here," said Cathy, "and it must be important."

Honesty can be a nuisance around a law office and must be weeded out remorselessly whenever it appears.

"Cathy," I said, "I am your employer and I say that I am not here."

She shrugged her shoulders and uncovered the receiver.

"Mr. McGuire says he's not here."

With the hot breath of law enforcement on my tail, a visit to the Sea Snakes was a must. So I bailed on Cathy and the telephones and set off on foot across the Marina to the offices of the Southern California Sea Pioneers.

You didn't need an appointment to see Hersh. Murray had told me he actually lived there, somewhere deep inside the enormous nautically designed clubhouse built with contributions intended for the benefit of the nonexistent young Pioneers. Hersh had furnished one of the meeting rooms a few years ago, and now more or less haunted the place. As usual, he was home, and a nice young lady in the reception area told me to wait a moment.

I had forgotten that Hersh's actual title with the Sea Pioneers was 'Commander,' so I had a blank moment when he appeared in full dress; a quasi-militaristic outfit replete with patches, medals, epaulets, and other bits and pieces hanging off here and there. He looked like the ranking military officer of a small South American country, with the kindly intelligent face of a veteran con man.

I knew his antics from before, when he called himself Horace Templeton and peddled investments in the Bank of Sark, a fictitious enterprise allegedly located on the Isle of Guernsey. Most people have no idea where that is. I think that was the idea. At the time, his activities goaded the Department of Justice and the SEC into a feeding frenzy from coast to coast which ended only after Hersh/Templeton had sold more than a million, eight hundred thousand dollars worth of bogus stock, (real money in those days), including one hundred and fifty thousand worth to the Chief of Police of a large middle western city. Later on, I heard he had sold stock to the Warden while serving a prison sentence.

Through the window behind him, the channel sparkled in the morning sun, and I could see activity on the Pioneer's private dock.

Hersh said, "So, McGuire, have you come here to donate that old harbor queen of yours?"

"When you go straight," I said.

This was the call and response of an exchange we had been having for years. I had long since stopped reacting to his reference to *Den Mother* as a harbor queen, which meant

37

an old decrepit vessel that can't go past the breakwater. *Den Mother* was no harbor queen, and I had the marine mechanic's paid bills to prove it. You had to understand his mind set; the Pioneers never paid any money for their boats. Everything was donated, and any boat Hersh saw could potentially be his with the stroke of a pen. An old securities violator like Hersh didn't take the stroke of a pen very seriously. He had a way of turning up in possession of particular boats he admired. As a boat owner, it made me nervous to be around him. He was like an overeager surgeon who might snatch your kid for organ transplants while your back was turned.

I filled Hersh in on my meetings with Murray and Doctor Rayburn, pointing out that the doctor was now dead. It could be assumed that the tax investigation would be closed and that Murray Markoff's imaginary boat would never see the light of day, but things felt unsettled. It seemed to me that Murray and the Southern California Sea Pioneers could both be at risk. It was hard to tell whether Hersh shared my concerns. He turned and pointed out the window.

"If you want Murray, he's right out there. Talking to the man from Washington."

Murray's colorful Hawaiian shirt made him easy to spot. He was standing on the foredeck of a large power cruiser tied at the Pioneer's dock. I said good-bye to Hersh and walked out of the club house and down the dock in the warm morning sunshine.

Murray was talking to a rumpled-looking man. There was no question that he was the man from Washington. He was clutching a heavy Government-issue brassbound leather briefcase of a style that went out in the Truman administration. He was wearing the kind of cut-rate suit you can only get from Louie's on Pennsylvania Avenue, the exclusive Washington D.C. source of cheap suits for agents of the IRS, the FBI, and for that matter the entire sweaty army of underpaid ill-tempered investigators and agents who, taken together, make this great nation what it is today.

I went on board and was introduced to the rumpled-looking man, whose name was Collins. It seemed clear that he was on board to check out Doctor Rayburn's donation to the Pioneers. It is true that the red-eye from DC can leave you looking rumpled, but Mr. Collins looked like he had spent a considerable amount of time in the type of clothes dryer that employs a revolving barrel. I watched as Murray took Collins over the boat's features, 'explaining' things to an obviously uncomprehending audience. Finally, we all retired to the salon, where we sat on nice new leather-upholstered built- in benches. The bulkheads were clean and bright, with the smell of new varnish; very nautical. On the bulkheads were prints of old sailing ships. I looked out the hatch at healthy young UCLA coeds rowing long racing shells. Mr. Collins' Truman-era briefcase crouched in the corner. I flashed on the idea that it was attack-trained and would fly at my throat at Collins' command. The rumpled-looking man was not the least bit fazed by the news of Doctor Rayburn's death.

"We don't get involved with things like that," he said. "Alive or dead he still has to pay his taxes." He made a useless attempt to straighten his collar. "At least this boat business looks OK."

Murray shot me a nervous glance on backchannel. I understood his concern; we were sitting on a beautiful 63-foot Pacemaker that Collins apparently believed was the boat Doctor Rayburn had donated to the Pioneers. Except it wasn't. It was the vessel *Pork Belly* and belonged to a friend of mine who had made a lot of money speculating in the commodity markets.

The man from Washington stood up and walked to the hatch. "I'll be back tomorrow," he said, "to review the paperwork."

Uh-oh; there was no way Murray could come up with documents; wrong year of manufacture, wrong owner, she was gas not diesel, and probably more. But, having little choice in the matter, we said goodbye to Mr. Collins and watched as he walked up the dock and into the parking lot, got into an entry-level rental car and drove off. Murray looked at me with an oddly intent expression and gestured with his chin; the rumpled looking man had forgotten his briefcase. Without hesitating Murray walked over to it, grabbed it and threw it through *Pork Belly's* outboard salon hatch into the channel, where it sank immediately. I was speechless. Murray made "don't worry' gestures at me with his hands.

Don't get stressed," he said, "I know what I'm doing. Mox nix. I've done this before. It works."

"Murray," I said, "They'll assassinate you. You'll do time. Why did you do that?"

"Trust me McGuire, I've done this before. Here's the way it works. The guy's a putz, right?" That sounded right. I nodded. "When he finds out the briefcase is gone he'll realize he's porked the poodle. He won't want his boss to find out. The other IRS agents are gonna laugh at him and now he won't get a raise. So the putz covers up by shutting down all the investigations in the briefcase. All he's gotta do is check a box on a form, get another briefcase, and he can start over on a new batch of people. Anyway, if you're that worried about the briefcase, wait, it'll come back up in two or three days."

"Come back up? You mean like a body?" He gave me a knowing look. "You think the briefcase will rot like a corpse and come floating up?"

I realized Murray didn't have a clear idea of what IRS agents carried in their briefcases. But there was no doubt in my mind that he was right about the result; Doctor Rayburn could rest in peace. His audit was over.

I realized there were dimensions to Murray that I had not appreciated before, and I told him so.

"You can do anything you want to," he said, "You just gotta have blimp balls, and use them."

"Blimp balls? You mean like the little thing that hangs down under the Goodyear Blimp?"

He shook his head. "No. Balls like blimps. Blimp balls."

6

It gets quiet down on the water. At night the boat is like an island. When I started living aboard I was surprised to find how safe it felt, how unlike my former home in Santa Monica. I had expected I would worry about the water under my new location. I could sink. I could be rammed by an out-of-control sailboat. Under the hull were twelve to twenty or so feet of water, depending on the tide. At the bottom of the water, ooze. In addition to all of the hazards of life on land, fish swim beneath. Like the Mafia threat, "you will sleep with the fishes." But I sleep over the fishes, and it brings an extra measure of peace. This only settled in on me after the first haul-out; after I had accepted the grotesque image of *Den Mother* out of the water, in the gigantic slings of the Travelift, then up on blocks.

In the boatyard I had inspected the hull and its through-hull fittings, considering the ways in which water could get into the boat. *Den Mother* had a history. She was a few years older then me, and as with all of us she had suffered many modifications and changes through the years. We found seven non-functional through-hull fittings below the waterline and the men at the boatyard sealed them up. By the time she was launched again I knew there were raw water intakes for my engines and generator, a pair of rudder glands and a pair of shaft logs with stuffing boxes. Once I had seen these fittings, and seen them get their maintenance as needed, I felt better. I felt safe. Fish may swim beneath me, but I would not sleep with them. When I was lucky, I slept with Maria, an altogether warmer and more cuddly proposition.

We lay in bed in the aft stateroom and listened to the evening sounds of Marina del Rey. A big excursion boat had started up C Basin from the Main Channel and we could just begin to hear the distant 'boom, boom, boom' of a rock band on board. Then the frenzied sounds of the passengers, dancing, hooting and boozing. Was it 'Dock of the Bay?' Yes, it was. As the boat came further up the Channel toward us it sounded more like the crowded, drunken cocktail lounge it was. Slowly, this throbbing nuisance powered by, reached the top of C Basin, turned, and started down again. The music stopped and the shrill, over-amplified voice of an MC could be heard. "Are you having a good time?" Evidently they were. Slowly the sounds faded as the boat moved down toward the Main Channel again. According to the Department of Beaches and Harbors, they could only carry on like that until nine-thirty. Loud, organized drunken boating stopped then, and only private disorganized efforts prevailed.

As we rested in the dark, things slowly quieted down. A sailboat went by on auxiliary power, a radio playing softly.

There is a reason why I live on a boat. Peace and quiet is the most precious commodity that money can buy, and it is hilarious that so many rich people have so little of it. Life on board *Den Mother* had brought me more peace and quiet than anyone would believe possible. And nobody knows we're here. So if people think it's weird that the honey boat pumps us out every week, that I worry about through-hull fittings, or that it can rock and roll a little in heavy weather, it's OK. In fact, it's perfect. If they knew how much fun Maria and I were having down here, they'd make it against the law.

I fell asleep thinking about Rigoberto Salas. *Señor.* Salas was a scavenger. He had been brained by a flying bag of trash while standing in a dumpster in Marina del Rey, practicing his profession. The person who had thrown the bag had not known that anyone was in there because Rigoberto was a small man and the sides of the dumpster were high enough to conceal him from view. The trash-tosser was only doing what he was supposed to; using the dumpster provided by the management of Leeward Marina for its tenants. Everything would have been fine, except for Rigoberto being in there looking for aluminum cans despite the sign on the dumpster warning against trespass. What a world; don't trespass in the garbage. *Señor* Salas didn't read English anyway, so his conscience was not burdened, as he was being brained, by an awareness of wrongdoing. The guy who threw the bag of trash was a drunk and the trash bag was full of empty bottles. It was the delivery of this chunky airmail that had concussed *Señor* Salas, induced a short period of unconsciousness and a subdural hematoma. And a nice black eye. Nice because it made a nice photograph. You couldn't see any of the rest.

Nobody disputed any of these facts. It was what to do with them that was the problem. Somehow it was always the other lawyers who got the great injury cases; the kind of case where the Sears truck squashes little Billy flat as a pancake in the crosswalk, with his lunchbox. Usually, when I get an injury case it's more like Rigoberto's. Kind of marginal. Four cards to a flush. I had tried the facts out on Maria.

She said "You think a Santa Monica jury is going to give money to some wetback who got hurt digging in their garbage?"

"That's harsh."

"You bet it is. My people come out here to the West Side to do gardening or wash dishes. We're supposed to be shoveling shit, not getting injured."

"Don't get excited."

"*No te claves*. You wanted my opinion? That's it."

We were sitting in *Den Mother's* aft cockpit at the end
of the day, the sun low in the sky. She had just come back
from downtown and hadn't had time to change; barefoot,
though, drinking white Bordeaux. I drank my wine and
looked at Maria's pretty little feet. She was the first woman I
had ever met who painted her toenails. I had been waging a
campaign against the toenail painting, with ambiguous
results. So far, she had agreed to paint toenails on the right
foot only, leaving the left *au nature*. She had offered this
compromise seriously, or so it seemed, but I was pretty sure
I was being made fun of. You take what you can get.

"Who told him to climb into a dumpster?" she said.
"Don't they have signs on them telling you not to get inside?"

I said "In Spanish?" She rolled her eyes.

"So you think it's a bustout?"

She held one leg out and peeled off a stocking. Little
red toenails winked at me. A flash of thigh. The sun had
almost disappeared. The surface of C Basin was darkening,
stirred by the late afternoon breeze. It was cooling off fast.

She said "Why do you do these cases? You told me it
was dead, the insurance companies aren't paying."

She was right. The personal injury business was on its
ass in Los Angeles. You couldn't settle anything.

"Habit, I suppose."

Maria said "You don't like to say no to people."

I thought about this. You can't run a law office like a
popularity contest. Sure, you might want your clients to like
you, but most lawyers would agree that the important thing
is to make money. I wondered, not for the first time, if I had
the correct mental attitude to practice law. Was I sufficiently
narrow-minded, egotistical, compulsive? Probably.

We sat and drank wine. Maria leaned back in her
chair, put the other leg up and peeled off another stocking. I
couldn't get over how exotic she looked, how brave.
Moments, I thought; life consists of moments. That was it, in
my opinion. No plan, no plot, just a sexy bare foot in the late

45

afternoon sun, a glass of wine.

"These are the cards life deals me," I said, "so I play them."

She turned her head toward me. "You just make that up?"

"Sort of."

"I told my mother, 'He's got a tongue like an angel; how he can talk.'"

"You told your mother I've got a tongue like an angel?" I made Groucho eyebrows at her.

"Oh, shut up."

She may have blushed, but it's hard to tell.

7

The next morning Larry Hayden called me at the office to tell me that the County D.A. was not going to file charges, but the bad news was that the U.S. Attorney's Office was going to proceed against us for an offense under Federal law; killing, injuring or harassing whales.

"Larry," I said, "a shark is not a whale."

"What the hell is that supposed to mean?"

"Did you read the arrest report?"

"Of course I did. The witness said you and your girlfriend were shooting at whales."

"But we had a Mako shark with bullet holes in it, right? Not a whale."

"According to the report your boat was too small to bring back a whale. How large was it?"

"The boat?"

"No, the whale."

It was time to stop thinking like a lawyer. My ass was on the line. I got in my car and drove up Pacific Coast Highway. I knew Maria and I had been about two miles off

Duke's Restaurant in Malibu when she shot the shark, so I pulled over when I thought I was a couple of miles south of Duke's and found a parking space.

The east side of PCH is pretty much a cliff from Santa Monica all the way to Cross Creek, in Malibu, and most of the ocean side is an unbroken wall of high-priced real estate. I had always wondered why anyone would want to live on this narrow margin between the cliffs and the sea, waiting to be wiped out by a storm, a landslide or a motorist, but there were many who didn't see it this way, and as a result there was almost no beach access from the street. I found my way down to the sand through a narrow passageway between two examples of the good life, and started walking north.

Few people actually go in the ocean in Southern California because the water is too cold, but the beach was well populated for a weekday, with sunbathers and joggers, a few surfers, despite the absence of surf, and here and there someone on horseback. I figured that anyone with binoculars and an attitude and the determination to drop a dime on an environmental criminal such as myself would have to have a local reputation, so I started asking people who looked like locals if they knew where the whale lady lived. This turned out to be a straight line and evoked more mirth than information, so I changed it to 'the environmental lady,' which didn't make any more sense but I didn't get laughed at either. I did this for a while, accumulating sand in my shoes and getting overheated. Just short of Duke's, I got a hit; a teenage boy wearing a bright blue and yellow wetsuit nodded and gestured over his shoulder.

"You mean her. Up there."

Up there was a newish beach house with wraparound picture windows and upper and lower redwood decks connected by a circular iron staircase. Fishnet and floats and other assorted beachcombing finds lay scattered on the lower deck, together with a few sand chairs and some skin-diving gear. The lower deck was two steps off the sand, and I walked up and said 'hello' loudly. A woman's voice from the upper deck said 'come up,' and I did.

49

Once upstairs I found myself facing a redheaded lady sunbather lying face down on a beach towel. In front of her lay an open book, some sort of a drink, a bowl of strawberries and what looked like a bowl of powdered sugar. As I stood there, she took a strawberry, dipped it in the powdered sugar, and ate it. She appeared to be nude. Her breasts were large enough to sort of hump up under her chin from her lying on them, and the tops of her breasts were lightly dusted with powered sugar from the strawberries. The light drift of white dust on her gently rounded breasts made me think of Christmastime department store window displays. All it needed was for a little Santa in a sleigh pulled by tiny reindeer to come across the gently swelling snowy hill...

"Did you come up here to stare at my boobs?"

I realized I had lost it. "No, I'm sorry, I was just thinking about Christmas when I was a kid."

She shifted slightly on her towel and looked puzzled. A small patch of snow slid off the top of one hill. I had spent some time at a local nude beach near Point Dume, and I was reminded that in a situation of social nudity, it is the clothed person who feels intimidated, not the naked one. Also, the Environmental Lady, if that was who she was, would not be entirely naked unless she stood up or turned over. At present, she was wearing a redwood deck. I thought I should explain myself.

"I'm the guy you called the Harbor Patrol about last weekend. My girlfriend and I were fishing out there when-"

She said "-I know what you were doing," working up a little righteous indignation. "This planet is poised on the edge of environmental catastrophe because of people like you. Are you sexually dysfunctional?"

I wasn't sure how to answer, but it wasn't necessary.

"Why don't you stay home on weekends and screw instead of going out and killing things?"

This had the sound of a well-rehearsed speech. There was no point trying to engage her statement on a literal level; to tell her that sex and fishing appealed to different

50

appetites, that most fisherman would rather fish than have sex, preferring to spend their time where they had at least a small amount of skill.

"I don't have a job," she said, "so I try to do something useful here at home, for the ecology, you know, the planet. It's our only home in the universe." She gestured out toward the intensely blue, flat calm bay. "I look out over the bay and all I can see are helpless animals suffering and dying, especially the dolphins and whales."

I knew we'd get to the whales soon enough. This was another one with an "I love whales" bumpersticker. Yeah, right.

YOU'VE SEEN THAT BUMPERSTICKER THAT SAYS 'I LOVE WHALES?' WELL, I LOVE LINGUINI WITH CLAM SAUCE, BUT I DON'T ADVERTISE IT ON MY BUMPER. I FIGURE IT'S NOBODY'S BUSINESS.

And she didn't wear fur, won't eat meat, won't go to Harlem in ermine and pearls, the whole deal. The most intensely irritating thing a person can do to me is to assume an attitude of moral superiority. I couldn't help myself. I jumped right in.

"How about the redwoods," I said, gesturing toward the deck. "Don't you believe in saving them?"

Her eyes flashed. I was playing in her backyard.

"If you'll let me put some clothes on I'll show you a certificate that all the timber used in these decks was taken from downed trees or from live trees removed in a scientific program of forest management."

So there, asshole. Was I somehow stopping her from putting on clothes? If so, should I keep on doing it? I was beginning to get a sexual buzz from standing there trying not to stare at her nicely tanned ass. The muscles looked good. Tennis, I thought. She must play tennis. I was unsure of the consequences of standing there too much longer.

"Look," I said, "There's something you need to know."

She looked skeptical. There was nothing she could

51

imagine that I could tell her, but that was the reason I was there.

"There are no whales out there," I continued. "This is summer. They migrate in the winter. I would never shoot one anyway, but it makes no difference. There aren't any out there."

She shook her head. She was irritated and I could see that she wanted to stand up but did not want to take off her certificated redwood deck. She pointed out toward the bay again.

"Just look out there. There's one right now."

I looked out toward the water in the direction she was pointing. The only thing I could see was a large kelp paddy floating about a hundred yards off the beach. Not a whale. Somehow I didn't feel like sharing this information. Give the public what it wants.

"Oh, right, what a surprise," I said. "Looks like a good size one. Must be lost."

"Sometimes," she said, "they get tangled up with the lobster pots."

This was a point at which it would have been very easy for me to get tagged for obstruction of justice. There are humorless folks down at the Federal Building who would frown on subjects of an investigation trying to influence potential witnesses to change their story. As Richard Nixon once said, it would be wrong. So, if the whales got tangled up with the lobster pots I would have to leave them there, lest I become tangled with them. Instead, I would try to be friendly.

"Isn't your husband a County prosecutor?"

"Yes. I'm sorry, I'm Kate Balducci. His name is Victor."

"I'm Tom McGuire. I'm a lawyer. I know Victor Balducci," I said, taking a fairly obvious gander at the upscale scenery. "I guess the County is paying them a little more than it used to."

She laughed. "My father gave us this house as a wedding present. Actually, he had it built for us. I'm sure you've heard of him, Franco Mandelbrot?"

Indeed I had. He was a developer who had scraped flat more Santa Monica mountaintops than any other human being in history, covering the hideous open wounds with equally hideous Mission-style homes. Hideous prices, too, but that was then. As I recalled, Mandelbrot's last assault on nature had been stopped by the collapse of the Southern California real estate market. The huge bulldozed terraces were still up there in the mountains above Malibu, awaiting the return of affluence to Southern California.

Now I understood the Evironmental Lady's reference to not having a job. She was rich. That was an environment I could get used to; just lay around in the buff, eat strawberries and make trouble for harmless shark fishermen. I guessed that a beach house in Malibu was spit in the ocean, so to speak, for a guy like Mandelbrot. And this was a particularly nice place. Through the picture windows facing the upper deck I could see Southwest style furniture and Indian rugs, as well as a display of what looked like Indian artifacts.

"Look, Mr. McGuire... can I call you Tom?"

This sounded pretty funny coming from a naked woman I had just met. Of course she could call me Tom.

"Tom, please understand this problem isn't about me, it's about you. Being a friend of the earth has its responsibilities."

I couldn't believe she could say something so breathtakingly asinine with a straight face, but there it was. I suddenly realized what I represented to her; I was a trophy. At some level she must have decided that if she could testify against us and get us convicted for shooting at whales she could hold her head up in environmental circles and dine out on the story for years.

Caught in the jaws of a predator a small animal goes limp. I said good-bye and walked down the circular staircase to the beach. The day was cooling, and the tide was coming in. I found my car and drove home.

8

The next morning there was a bigger, better whale story in the *Times*. Evidently, whales were having a lot of problems; gillnets, Japanese and Scandinavian outlaw whalers, pollution, and, so the *Times* would have it, me. Thank you Harry Hatcher. He wrote that I had refused to comment; the classic modern-day badge of shame; 'no comment,' evoking news footage of some poor schmuck hiding his face in his Borsalino as they lead him in to get measured for a striped suit. Something nasty was coming, I could feel it, but there was no time to worry; today I had to take Moe to meet the Feds.

Moe was a huge bodybuilder I had met while working out at World Gym in Venice. He was a pleasant, essentially harmless guy, with a bland disposition, a head of frizzy orange hair and blue eyes as vacant as a patch of empty blue sky. It was a shock when he called me to say he had been arrested by the Secret Service for counterfeiting. How could

Moe have committed such a complicated crime? He explained that he had 'raised' a two-dollar bill by cutting off its corners and gluing on the corners of a twenty-dollar bill. I guess you get four twenties and use one corner from each, so nobody will notice. Moe then attempted to pass the raised bill at the grocery store on the corner of the block on which he had lived all his life, for a clear profit of eighteen dollars. Late that night Secret Service agents in overcoats (it was July) arrested him at the front door of his home. Only a bodybuilder could get into such trouble.

I had always believed that over-development of the muscles of the neck put pressure on the carotid arteries, cutting off the supply of blood to the brain, and that was why bodybuilders were inclined to be slow. Maybe it was simply that nobody with any brains would spend so many hours in a gym trying to make himself look like the Michelin Man. That's what I thought, anyway. Back then, nobody realized it was a step on the road to becoming Governor of California. Go figure.

Anyway, there we were, Moe and me, at the U.S. Attorney's Office at 312 North Spring Street, the home of the Fed and the land of the scared; the counterfeiter and his mouthpiece.

A short interview with Moe convinced the young Assistant United States Attorney assigned to the case that my client was too dim to be a danger to anyone. After some palaver, we settled on a Brooklyn Plan, which essentially means that we all agreed to go away and not bother each other forever. Or, as they say in Brooklyn, fuggedaboudit. No charges would be filed. Moe thought I was God. The only thing was, as we walked up the corridor toward the elevators I looked past someone leaving an inner office and for an instant through a closing door I saw Doctor Rayburn. He wasn't dead, or at least he didn't look dead. He was sitting in a swivel chair, talking to somebody I couldn't see. He didn't see me.

I thought about this all afternoon. I couldn't wait to tell Maria when she turned up at the boat after work. Her reaction was not what I expected.

"So maybe he's not dead," she said. "Big deal. You people are too logical, you think in absolutes. Dead, not dead."

"Wait a minute. When you say 'you people,' who do you mean?"

She ignored this. "It's like the woman who says she saw us shoot a whale. She saw a whale, we didn't."

"Thank you Carlos Castaneda."

"*De nada.*"

I thought, something as big as a whale, it's not metaphysics. You ought to be able to make up your mind if it's real or not. But before I could express this thought Maria had disappeared forward to the galley, and was rummaging around in the refrigerator.

It had been quite some time after I met Maria that I realized she had two degrees from UCLA. In the beginning, she had played it straight San Gabriel Valley local girl. She had been wary of me, an Irish-Jewish boy from New York City, more exotic to her than she had appeared to me, and from a place she had never been. Did I think of her then as Carmen Miranda, dancing the conga with a flowing skirt and fruit on her hat? You know, 'ay-yi-yi-yi-yi I like you varrrr-y much.' Yeah, of course I had thought that. Just a little.

By now what might have been a culture clash had become a game. Her game. When I looked for intuition, sometimes I got logic. When I insisted there was a distinction between dead and alive, she became a *bruja*, a witch woman, and I got the Wisdom of the Ancients. Part of my respect for her came from a feeling I had that on some level she might be a bigger wiseass than I was.

Soon Maria returned from the galley with baguette, *Crottin de Chavignol* and smoked salmon. World-class canapé fixings. A bulwark against depression and despair.

"Ok then," I said, "figure this out. I've got to find some way to stop this whale business. It sounds like a joke, but we could lose at trial. You can't take that chance. Only idiots go to trial. If there was some way I could dig up some dirt on these people..."

Maria arranged the goodies on a large platter. She looked thoughtful as she sliced the baguette.

"If you want to find dirt," she said, "look in the garbage."

I was turning that over, wondering if it was an old Hispanic saying, when it dawned on me. Rigoberto Salas, the dumpster diver. Was he in good enough shape to go back to work? I had the telephone number of his aunt, and I gave it to Maria, my designated Spanish speaker and guru.

9

Cathy buzzed me and said that Hersh was on the line. This was odd; Hersh never called. Like the practiced con man that he was, he always preferred that you be the one calling him; the one who wanted something. But not today. Today Hersh had a problem.

"I wouldn't bother you with this unless it was important," he said. "We've had a visit from a Police Detective named Radovich. He's investigating the murder of Doctor Rayburn, and he's really leaning on us. On us! Can you imagine the Sea Pioneers committing murder?"

In truth I could not; forgery, fraud, maybe, but not murder. Anyway, it was backwards.

"The last time I heard this song," I said, "it was Murray telling me that Doctor Rayburn was threatening to kill *him*. How'd it get turned around? "

"I'll tell you how. Radovich says that Rayburn's nurse says that all that Doctor could talk about in the weeks before he died was Murray and the Pioneers, and how much he hated them, and how much he wished he had Murray back on the operating table, and what he would do to him if he could. Radovich says maybe we killed him to protect ourselves."

'The Proctologist's Revenge' was a sobering concept. I didn't think it was a good idea to tell Hersh about my sighting of Doctor Rayburn at the Federal Building, because I didn't understand what it meant. I remembered Maria's observation that it didn't make a lot of difference whether he was dead or not. Could that possibly be so?

Hersh and I agreed that I would represent them in connection with Radovich's investigation. I told Hersh that my next call would be to Radovich, but I lied. My next call was to Larry Hayden at the U.S. Attorney's office. Larry wasn't there, and it was late afternoon before he returned the call. He didn't react to my account of the Rayburn murder investigation. I realized he wasn't going to show me his, so I showed him mine.

"The problem I have with all this, Larry..."

"Yes?"

"...the problem is that Doctor Rayburn isn't dead."

"He isn't?" It didn't slow him down at all. "That should give you a great bargaining position. You could plead your clients to a lesser offense, you know, manslaughter or something."

"That's funny, Larry, but I saw Doctor Rayburn the other day on the twelfth floor of the Federal Building. The U.S. Attorney's Office, where you work. Where you're sitting right now."

My hope that this would get his attention was not realized.

"You were down here? Why didn't you stop in?"

"I'll come down there right now and buy you dinner if you'll tell me why your people faked Rayburn's death, and what you're doing with him."

There was a moment of silence. I had gotten Larry's attention at last.

"No," he said, "I've got bowling tonight." A pause. "You know, there are people who think they see Elvis, too."

"Not at the U.S. Attorney's Office they don't."

"Tom, if I was a doctor I'd tell you to take two aspirins and call me in the morning. I don't know what to say about these visions of yours. Why don't you take me to dinner at one of those neat places at the beach you used to brag about? We could talk."

I wanted to give Larry an opportunity to think about the Rayburn business so I told him I would get back to him. I was about to call Radovich when Cathy said there were two people to see me; a man and a little boy. I walked up to the reception area to take a look and it was Rigoberto Salas and his son. In another life Rigoberto could have been a jockey. The man couldn't have weighed a hundred and ten pounds. He was shy; self-effacing to the point of invisibility, as if he made a career of not being noticed. A small, dark, anonymous man in anonymous clothes who did not meet your gaze. I remembered part of a poem from my childhood:

> As I was going up the stair
> I met a man who wasn't there

The little boy more than made up for it. He was a cheerful seven or eight years old, all smiles and baby fat, in a bright blue Dodgers windbreaker and the kind of expensive battery-powered sport shoes that flash when you walk. He was carrying several small plastic action figures; spacemen, by the look of them. He did the talking.

"My papa brought these things for you," he said.

Señor Salas held out his parcels. He was carrying a shopping bag half filled with dirty-looking papers, and a burlap sack. He handed me the sack and I looked inside. It was full of bones. Old, brown bones. Right on top there was a skull. It was a bag of people bones. I looked up with alarm. The little boy was smiling at me, waiting for words of praise, of thanks. *Señor* Salas was looking out the window but I could tell he was proud of his efforts. There was no way I was

60

going to disappoint them.

"Hey, this is great," I said, with more enthusiasm than I felt. "Thank you. Please ask your father where these..." I gestured at the sack "...came from."

The boy looked puzzled.

"Papa got them for you." There was a short dialogue in Spanish. "At the beach. The house at the beach. What your *esposa* asked him."

I didn't think the bones came from a dumpster, but I realized Maria was going to have to talk to Rigoberto before it would get clarified. I thanked them both and as I handed Rigoberto a fifty-dollar bill I reflected that I had more or less conspired to steal human remains. There undoubtedly were laws against it.

After they were gone I closed my office door and locked it. I cleared off my desk and took the bones out, one by one. There were a lot of them. There were actually three skulls, one nearly complete with a lower jaw and a few worn-looking teeth. Most of them were long bones, probably legs or arms, with an assortment of others I wasn't sure about. It's not something you study in law school. They were all dark brown, and smooth, like river stones. My impression was that they had been buried in the ground for a long time. They smelled like stones and they were clean, as if they had been carefully washed.

The intercom buzzer gave me a moment of pure panic before I realized the door was locked and I didn't have to hide the bones. I told Cathy to hold my calls and spent a half-hour researching the law. Bone law.

Assuming that the bones were merely human remains, it turned out it was illegal for me to possess them. It was illegal for someone to have removed them from the ground, if that was where they came from. If the bones were ancient remains of Native Americans, they were protected by elaborate and complex Federal laws. At this point I started thinking about whales. Where in the Federal penal system would they put a man who was both a killer of whales and a despoiler of Native American graves? On the other hand, I was not going to ask *Señor* Salas to take the bones back where he got them. So I put them back in the sack, put the whole thing in an empty file drawer and went home. I was walking down my dock before I realized I hadn't looked at the papers in the shopping bag.

10

As soon as I got on board I called Maria at work and asked her to try and reach Rigoberto through his aunt. I needed to figure out how they had turned up with the bag of bones. Twenty minutes later she called back. The aunt knew all about it. Most probably the whole community knew; how often do you find a bag of bones? I mean a real one, not a metaphor. The bag had been in the back of a little blue truck parked in the Environmental Lady's driveway. The papers in the shopping bag had come from the trashcan. I figured if I drove up there right away I would have a chance of spotting the truck, so I did.

It was a little blue Chevy pickup, with 'Mandelbrot Development' lettered on the doors, over a tasteful graphic of a palm tree and a mountain, and a telephone number, which I copied down. At that point I recalled the Indian artifacts I had noticed while standing on the upper deck of the Environmental Lady's beach house. I thought I knew where the bones were coming from, and I drove further up Pacific Coast Highway and turned right at Big Rock, up into the mountains.

It had been years since I had been up there, but it was still refreshingly wild. That's L.A., a thin veneer of civilization but turn a corner and you're going up a brushy canyon full of wildlife, human and animal. I remembered and found roads I had not been on for ten years, and finally an overgrown bulldozer track on which I gingerly drove. Overgrown brush scraped at the sides of my car as I bumped along. Finally, I stopped at the edge of a vast scraped-off plain; the last tango of Mandelbrot Development, smothered in the cradle by the real estate collapse. A large weathered sign announced an opportunity to appear at a hearing at the L.A. County Department of Regional Planning, to consider the proposed subdivision submitted by Mandelbrot Development. Two hundred and twenty units, a park, a pool, a community center. Spanish Mission-style charm up the wazoo.

Marksmen had been at work; the sign was riddled with bullet holes. The paint had faded along with the dreams of Mandelbrot Development. Nothing was going to be built here in the near future. A gently rolling series of lightly wooded plateaus had been tormented and beaten into bare terraces, somewhat eroded by winter rains, and tufted here and there with grass, here and there a beer can, a light drift of broken glass, the odd discarded condom.

Far below was the blue ocean and the long horseshoe of beachfront stretching from Point Dume to Palos Verdes. It would be nice to have a house up here as long as you didn't mind coyotes carrying off your small children and household pets, and the fickle Pacific Coast Highway's periodic flooding and landslides.

I walked around looking for signs of excavation. There was no evidence that anyone had been doing any digging since the bulldozers left, more than a year ago by the looks of things. If Franco Mandelbrot or his daughter, the Environmental Lady, had found ancient Indian remains here,

65

it had not been recently.

The light was fading and I didn't want to drive on dirt roads in the dark. I threaded my way back to blacktop, and thence to civilization, such as it was. Twenty minutes later I was walking down the dock toward my boat, noticing that in the cheerful picture framed by *Den Mother's* dockside salon hatch, the classic interior of a nice old Chris, there was a stranger, seated taking to Maria. She had on her best 'do I have to do this' look. She was not having a good time. The guy looked to me like a plainclothes detective. He introduced himself to me. He was a plainclothes detective; it was the return of Detective Radovich.

A lot of things ran through my mind at once. Should I tell Detective Radovich that Doctor Rayburn was alive, that I had seen him, that Larry's people at the U.S. Attorney's Office were somehow keeping him, that they faked his death? How many of these things were true? It sounded like a lot of luncheon meat. All I would accomplish by telling Radovich about it would be a total loss of credibility. On the other hand, I was Murray's lawyer. Hersh's too. Larry was right; Rayburn's continued existence was the perfect defense. We didn't kill him because he isn't dead. Could they prove Doctor Rayburn was dead if I couldn't prove he wasn't? Just then I remembered that I had a sack of human remains stashed in my office. I don't like confusion; it makes me uncomfortable. It puts the kibosh on my *savoir faire.*

Radovich was sitting on the only comfortable chair in the salon, apparently enjoying the late forties ambience of my boat. Maria had made him a cup of coffee. Cop stereotypes don't work well in Los Angeles. Although he was wearing the regulation Sears Roebuck polyester sport jacket, white socks, black shoes, Detective Radovich looked more like an ageing surfer than a cop; tall, fit, and tan; blond with just a little gray around the edges. Everyone looks fit and tan around here, even junkies.

"Well, Detective Radovich," I said, "It's certainly a pleasure to see you."

I always try to be extra cordial with the police. They

expect hostility, so that way you can at least try to break even. He looked completely at ease, as if he did most of his investigations on boats.

"Sorry to barge in, McGuire." Was this a pun? "I was on the next dock over and I realized you were out here on the end tie. I was meaning to talk to you anyway, about Mr. Markoff and his boss."

The next dock over was full of boats owned by various law enforcement types, and was commonly known as the FBI dock. Maria was down in the galley, looking busy but listening.

"You want to ask me about Doctor Rayburn, go ahead," I said, "but I was just retained this afternoon and I'm not sure I have anything to offer."

"Sure you do, McGuire. For openers you could tell me why you visited Rayburn's office the morning of the day he died."

Holy kazoozis, I had forgotten. My name must have been in his appointment book. It sometimes takes me so long to see the obvious.

"A hemorrhoid, Detective."

It was pure inspiration. Why else would I visit a proctologist? The words hung heavily in the air, like obese homing pigeons without a place to roost.

"It's like a conscience," I said. "Lawyers tend to get them as they get older."

Fortunately, the Detective's back was to the galley and he couldn't see Maria's silent laughter. I thought that he wouldn't want to hear much more about my medical problems. I tried to make sure.

"You know how it is, I sit a lot in my line of work, and it gets-"

"-Ok, sure, you don't have to draw me a picture." This novel idea had not occurred to me. "It's just quite a coincidence," he went on, "you see Doctor Rayburn just a few hours before he's killed just a few blocks from where you keep your boat, then you get hired by guys he was pissed off at on account of some tax dodge."

"I see your point, Detective, but truthfully it was my ass that brought me to Doctor Rayburn. I believe he's the best on the West Side. I guess now I'll have to go elsewhere. It's been a terrible problem. I have to sit in Court for hours on those hard wooden chairs." It was working. "I'll bet it's the same with cops, sitting around for hours." That did it. He was out the hatch and on the dock saying good-bye.

"Thanks for the coffee. I'll be in touch. We'll want your clients' cooperation."

"Of course you will," I said. "Just let me talk to them. I'll let you know. By the way, where was Doctor Rayburn transported from the scene of the crime?" I knew the answer to this question, but I wanted to hear him say it.

Radovich frowned. "Funny you should ask," he said. "I can't figure it out. The guy gets nailed around the corner from Marina Mercy Hospital, in the Marina, and he winds up DOA at the Veterans Administration Hospital in West L.A., miles away. Ain't that a pisser?" He paused. "Listen, your people don't look so good here. Rayburn's capped pulling his car into the parking lot in front of the Sea Pioneers clubhouse. We know he was angry with the Pioneers for fucking up his taxes, and I think he was on his way to have a confrontation with them. Then there's the car, a great big Mercedes sedan with custom paint and a personal plate with a word that means 'ass' in French. It's gotta stand out like a wedding prick. Not your typical carjacking target. And your friend Hersh is the registered owner of several firearms, including a shotgun, which he told me he couldn't find when I asked to see it. Hersh has a file at Interpol. He's a world-class slimebag. And his buddy Markoff was running errands for bookmakers and loansharks in New York when I was learning to pull my pud in West Covina."

It was the most I had heard him say at one time. He glowered at me. I shrugged. He turned to go. I watched him walk up to the sea wall, and over to the FBI dock, and I reflected on the large amount of covert law enforcement activity that goes on in Marina del Rey.

For starters, you've got the anti-smuggling task force,

Operation Pacific, which is made up of detachments from almost every enforcement organization you can think of; FBI, DEA, the U.S. Coast Guard, L.A. County Sheriff's Harbor Patrol, State and local police agencies and California Department of Fish and Game. And all this without any visible presence. No little office with "Operation Pacific" on the door, no uniforms, nothing. Of course, it is impossible to go out the Main Channel after dark without one or more parked cars suddenly illuminating your boat with their headlights. And Bobby Baxter's sad story of his botched marlin trip wasn't the first time I had heard of fishermen encountering law enforcement while peacefully trying to kill fish. One visible presence, however, was the U.S. Marshal's Service. For reasons I had never been able to figure out, their cars were around the Marina a lot. It was the U.S. Marshal's Service that ran the Federal Witness Protection Program, an institution that had always worried me. Consider it; a Federal bureaucracy devoted to blurring the lines between fantasy and reality. An official cornucopia of false people, of bogus histories. Considering that Doctor Rayburn was supposed to be dead but wasn't, it seemed reasonable to me that he had starred in a street theater production put on by the U.S. Marshal's Service, in which his disappearance was disguised by a fake carjacking and murder. But it was not fair to leave loose ends; to let well-intentioned police detectives investigate more or less innocent tax fraud artists for a murder that didn't happen. President Nixon said it best; 'it would be wrong.'

11

The next morning I called the Veterans Administration Hospital in West L.A. and spoke to a very helpful person in Records. Doctor Rayburn had been pronounced dead on arrival there on the evening Maria and I had seen the carjacking story on TV.

The Very Helpful Person faxed me a copy of the death certificate, a confidential document I was not supposed to have. It indicated that the body had been released to the L.A. Coroner for autopsy. Another call confirmed my recollection that autopsy reports are also not available to the public, but I did learn that after the autopsy the Coroner's office had released the body to the Neptune Society, an organization that arranges for cremation and scattering of ashes at sea. Bake and shake. There go the DNA comparisons.

The death certificate was not remarkable. It described a male Caucasian who could have been Rayburn, dead of a

70

massive shotgun wound. Why are white people described as Caucasian only when they're arrested or dead? I did get a personal detail from the Neptune Society. The body had a tattoo of an anchor and the initials USN on the upper right arm. Rayburn had not struck me as a Navy man, but who knows? I called Murray and left a message at the Pioneers. He called me back within the hour.

"In the Navy?" Murray was indignant. "From this I never heard. The way he talked to me, if he was ever on a boat in his life it was the Staten Island Ferry. Not a chance, McGuire, who's telling you this?"

"Well, he had a Navy tattoo. You know, an anchor and the initials USN."

"Phony Baloney, boychik, they're talking about a different guy. Rayburn was Jewish, it couldn't have been him."

"You lost me. What's his religion have to do with it?"

"Jews don't get tattoos, dummy. If you have a tattoo you can't be buried in a Jewish cemetery."

"Who says?"

"My Mother, the Bible, what's the difference? Everybody knows. Jews don't get tattoos. If he had a tattoo he wasn't Jewish. *Fertig.*"

"How do you know he was Jewish, Murray, Rayburn doesn't strike me as a Jewish name?"

"Oh stop with this Jewish name stuff, Tom. Your name's McGuire. Your mother was Jewish. Are you Jewish?"

I repeated Lenny Bruce's line: "If necessary." He ignored me.

"The man was Jewish," he continued. "I talked Yiddish with him. Believe me he didn't learn it at Berlitz. He could talk kitchen Yiddish, a few phrases, some words. I kidded him about it. But with a tattoo? No. You've got the wrong guy."

Murray had the right idea. It was something I knew a lot about from my childhood. Who would expect a little freckle faced kid named McGuire to speak Yiddish? My mother. She had loved my father and never worried that he

71

was Irish and Catholic, although the rest of her family had been ready to kill them both. But she remained passionate about her traditions. I was to be the torchbearer, it appeared, of the Yiddish language. My father was opposed; said it was old-fashioned. "Who's he going to speak Yiddish to, the butcher?" "He'll speak Yiddish with me," she answered him. And I did, when my Father was at work.

So after all I did speak Yiddish to the butcher, to his enormous amusement, and to the Grandparents on my mother's side while they were alive. And to my mother. As I got older I gradually became aware of the cultural dynamite I was handling. If you're a kid and you say something in Yiddish to an old Jew from anywhere in Central Europe, you are evoking another world, opening a box of memories as big as the planet.

I remember a joke my mother used to tell about a Jewish grandmother speaking Yiddish to her grandson on a bus in Tel Aviv. The little boy keeps answering her in Hebrew and, each time, she admonishes him to speak Yiddish. Finally, a passenger interrupts and points out that they are in Israel, where Hebrew is the language of the country, and asks why she insists that the little boy speak Yiddish. She says "I don't want him to forget he's a Jew."

So, if Murray was right, Rayburn was Jewish and the guy with the anchor tattoo was someone else. A body double. If Larry Hayden's people at the witness protection program staged Rayburn's murder, then they had to come up with a corpse to take to the hospital. A bullet-ridden corpse. It was creepy. Did the poor guy die of gunshot wounds, or was he dead when they shot him?

I made one more phone call.

"Larry, you've got a lot of explaining to do. There's something that doesn't add up about the Rayburn killing."

"Oh goody. I've been waiting for this. You're going to invite me to dinner, right?"

I invited him to dine with me that night, at Chinois on Main, in Ocean Park, my very favorite restaurant on Earth. When I die, it is my wish to be buried at Chinois on Main. I don't know how they might feel about such a request. They have always been very obliging in the past. Maybe just my ashes in an urn on a high shelf behind the bar. It's not asking so much, considering what I've spent there over the years.

True, the tables are tiny and set too close together. The din is horrendous, and it's very expensive, but it's a great place and it brings out the best in me. I agree with the late, great Ring Lardner when he said 'I have known what it is to be hungry, but I always went right to a restaurant.'

We got to sit at the counter. It's funny, sitting at the counter at Chinois on Main is supposed to happen when there are no more tables. A kind of bleachers, a Siberia, in the eyes of some customers. To me, the counter is the best show in town, because you get to sit and watch six or eight world-class chefs cook at the top of their form. In white uniforms, under bright lights, at enormous stoves, refrigerators, counters. It is at once violent and restrained. A carefully controlled chaos. And if once in a while a lobster escapes the cleaver or a small fire occurs while the dessert chef is finishing off the *crème brûleé,* who cares? Life is full of accidents.

We struggled to communicate amidst the roar of conversation and kitchen noises. The next man over at the counter was telling his companion a story, at the top of his voice, about what his New York cabdriver had said and done to the other cabdriver, complete with large expressive gestures. I was afraid he was going to knock over my bottle of Pellegrino water. Larry seemed pleased with his calamari salad, though he insisted on calling it fried squid.

Finally, we had worked the whole deep-fried catfish down to bare bones. There was nothing coming but the *crème brûleé,* although I was considering a glass of Black Muscat dessert wine. A cigar was of course out of the question. In today's climate of opinion a cigar in a restaurant would get you three to five in the Big House, which reminded me of something.

"Larry old buddy, what do you think the boys in the

exercise yard are going to say when I tell them I'm in for shooting at whales?"

Larry looked embarrassed. He poured the last of a nice bottle of Sancerre I had generously ordered.

"Whales are sexy, Tom, I have no control over this file." So now it was a file. "It's being run out of Washington. There's a whole environmental section at Justice, and the trouble is we've had this marine mammal statute on the books for years and it's hard to find cases to prosecute. People are interested in the environment, and they want to see their Government do something about it. I can't help it. Whales are the teddy bears of the environmental movement. Everybody loves them."

I thought of the Environmental Lady, with the powdered sugar boobies. I felt like Alice in Wonderland.

I said, "Did you know that Jews don't get tattoos?"

Larry stopped eating. He looked at me funny.

"What did you say?"

"Jews don't get tattoos, Larry. Your people at the V.A. got some poor dead sailor to stand in for Doctor Rayburn. Someone with a Navy tattoo. Do you realize there's a police detective trying to put my clients in jail for murdering somebody you people are hiding?" At this point I had the feeling that diners on both sides of us were listening. My dinner companion looked uncomfortable.

"Jesus, Tom, can't you keep your voice down?"

"No, dammit," I said a little louder.

Larry looked grim, then looked away from me as he spoke.

"Would it make a difference if I told you the whale thing is negotiable if you forget Rayburn? I'm not saying we did anything wrong, but it could have the potential of embarrassing the Department if you stay out there howling in the wilderness."

Now things were getting interesting. I gestured for our waiter. Forget dessert wine; this deserved a brandy.

"You're telling me Maria and I can walk for the whales if I let Hersh and Markoff take a fall?"

74

"Not exactly. Well, maybe. What we don't want are people saying that Doctor Rayburn isn't dead. You know, the integrity of the whole witness protection program-"

"-Integrity?"

"Aw, cut it out. You know what I mean."

"So, let me make sure I understand you. My clients, Hersh and Markoff, are being investigated for the murder of a person who is not actually dead, but I'm not supposed to go around saying this because it might embarrass the Department?"

Larry sighed and shook his head. He said, "I told them it wouldn't work."

My brandy arrived. He looked at it wistfully. "Look," he said, "let me excuse myself for a moment. I've got to make a call."

He got up and walked toward the back of the restaurant. Things had taken a curious turn. Confronted with this new information, my impulse was to let it percolate for a few days before deciding what to do. It was not to be. As we left the restaurant men in overcoats (it was August) approached me on either side, asked my name, and arrested me for violating Title 16 United States Code, Section something or other, which I assumed was the Marine Mammal Protection Act. Larry was nowhere to be seen. They took me to a four-door white sedan double parked in front of the restaurant, and put me in the backseat. On the door I noticed an emblem and the words U.S. Marshal's Service.

When we got downtown to the Metropolitan Detention Center one of my captors casually informed me that Maria was also in custody. So that was why Larry had left the counter to make a phone call. Some Larry; he baits a trap with a hundred-and-fifty-dollar restaurant meal that I pay for. Some Larry.

It was ten p.m. by the time I bailed out, which allowed me ample time to reflect on the situation. My first concern was for Maria, who was nowhere to be seen. Usually, if the U.S. Attorney's office wanted to arrest a client of mine, they would let me know and I would come downtown with the alleged perpetrator when Court was in session, and surrender him before a U.S. Magistrate. My bail bondsman would know about it in advance, and it would be a simple do-si-do in and out, allowing only for the time it took for them to do the booking. Clearly, Maria and I were being given a taste of the lash.

Well, it's one thing to roust a couple of law-abiding citizens. Making the charges stick in court would be much more difficult. I wouldn't be anxious to put the Environmental Lady on the witness stand if I were the Government. They'd have to get her to put on clothes, for one thing. If she started making speeches about the environment, which she was sure to do, some jurors might think she was strange. What she thought she heard, and saw through binoculars, was happening in and around a small open boat at least two miles out at sea. I knew from experience it's almost impossible to see anything through binoculars under those circumstances. Also, The Harbor Patrol had photographs of the Mako shark carcass with bullet holes in it.

If we shot at a whale, nobody could prove we had hit one, but apparently we could also be convicted of merely 'annoying' a whale. Tell me how you annoy an animal bigger than a Winnebago that lives under water? Who would testify that the whale had been annoyed? What if it had been amused? Bored? It would make an interesting trial. The biggest threat to me, apart from widespread ridicule, might be from the State Bar of California. Lately this venerable institution had been wallowing in an orgy of self-flagellation, disciplining, suspending and even disbarring lawyers for a variety of bad conduct unrelated to the practice of law. This would be likely to include violations of the Marine Mammal Protection Act. On the other hand, a lot of clients I've worked for would probably want to be represented by a lawyer who shot whales.

The Metropolitan Detention Center is a cheerless but efficient building of the kind that Albert Speer used to turn out for the Third Reich. I waited in the lobby until eleven, when Maria emerged. She was angry and tired, but appeared undamaged by her abduction. We took a sixty-dollar cab ride to Ocean Park to get my car, which was still sitting where the parking valet had left it behind Chinois on Main.

As we drove down to the Marina from Ocean Park I reflected that, by spotting Doctor Rayburn at the U.S. Attorney's office, I had caught the US Government with its metaphorical pants around its ankles, and Uncle Sam was now officially mad at us. As I saw it, there were two big questions. One was how to neutralize the Environmental Lady and destroy Larry's case against Maria and me. The second was how to prove Doctor Rayburn was alive. There were a few minor issues, like for example that Larry Hayden needed a good smack in the chops, in my opinion, but there was no time. When Maria and I got back to the boat I pulled the curtains on the dock side and turned off the phone. We slept

12

I was awake but I didn't know why. Maria lay beside me, snoring softly. I assumed that something had woken me so I lay quietly and listened. Dock lines creaking; that's ok. Soft little noises from various places inside the boat; I could never figure out what made them, but they were familiar. An occasional clicking sound against the outside of the hull, also familiar, cause unknown. From down-channel the ragged cry of a Night Heron. All familiar sounds, but something drew me out of bed and forward to the forepeak.

From out of the forward channel-side porthole I could see someone in an inflatable raft, doing something to my boat. I stifled an impulse to shout out the porthole. With pulse and respiration going bananas I walked over to the electric panel and turned the lever that brought twelve-volt power to the control bridge, then tiptoed up the ladder to the bridge and pressed an illuminated button over the label "anchor release." This gadget had cost me three hundred dollars when I had tried to devise an approach to single-handing *Den Mother*. Then, my friends had laughed at such an effete refinement. Now from the bow there were some very satisfying developments; a rattle of chain, a cry of surprise or pain, a crunching noise, and then the sound of more chain passing over the chain roller. I could hear what sounded like somebody thrashing around in the water.

I ran out on deck and saw that my anchor had obediently dropped off its bracket at the bow, smashing through the floor of the inflatable, and continued on to the bottom of the channel. The raft was full of water and paint, and there was paint in the water. Off the bow on the channel side someone in a black wetsuit was swimming away slowly. I ran out to the foredeck and managed to snag him with the boat hook I kept on the bow, and there we were for a moment. He was much too heavy for me to haul out of the water, and he couldn't get free. He seemed to have the use of only one arm. I think he wanted to curse at me but didn't want to make noise, so he whispered in a nasty way. Or so it seemed. If I could have gotten down onto the dock I could have pulled him in, but the boathook was much too short to allow this maneuver from the foredeck, so I settled for shouting "Help, Police" a few times. Lights went on in nearby boats, and Maria appeared on deck. She pointed at me and started to say something. I told her to call the Harbor Patrol, but someone must have done that already because I could hear the siren of the Harbor Patrol boat approaching from the Main Channel.

The Harbies must have had bad directions because they didn't slow down as they approached. Instead they continued past us at speed, further up C Basin. I stood transfixed at the bow of my boat and watched helplessly as their wake, a three-foot wall of water, advanced toward us. In an instant we were rolling violently at the dock. Nothing on board was stowed for sea travel and I heard the sound of glass breaking and things falling inside my boat. The man in the wet suit was no longer snagged at the end of my boat hook. Then the Patrol boat was back, ten feet off my bow.

Suddenly a searchlight was trained on me and an amplified voice said "Put your hands in the air." I dropped the boat hook and slowly did as I was told. I said "Don't shoot."

It took me and the Harbies quite a while to sort things out. The inflatable had a hole in the bottom where my eighty-pound CQR anchor had gone through on its way to the bottom. Worse, it was my inflatable, taken from its accustomed place at the sea wall. The raft was full of red paint and an empty paint can that identified it as Z-Spar Red Marine Enamel. Quality stuff. Costs more than good Scotch. Red paint had gotten on my boat at the water line on the channel side, and, the *coup de gras*, the intruder had written 'Whale Killer' in ragged red letters under my bow. The friend of the Earth who had accomplished all this ruin was not to be found. The Harbies called him a 'humainiac.' I liked that. During the two or three hours it took to sort everything out an image kept flickering at the edge of my recollection; Maria standing on the foredeck in her bathrobe, a pistol in her hand. Had that really happened?

It was after two o'clock the next afternoon before I was anywhere near operational. It was hard for me to accept the idea that somebody had vandalized my boat. To me a boat is a person. It has always mystified me that people will sink or torch boats for insurance payoffs. Once someone told me he had sold his boat to a movie company so they could blow it up on film. It made as much sense to me as somebody taking money to blow up his grandmother. As the reality of it sank in, my bafflement began to be replaced by anger, but I think Maria was madder than I was.

"You should have woken me up first," she said. "Why didn't you?"

"You might have shot him." The memory was clear to me now; while I had been fishing in the water with the boathook, Maria had been standing behind me holding the .357. Looking for a clear shot?

"Not necessarily."

"For Christ sake, you can't just shoot at somebody floating around in the water. I'd already knocked him out of the raft with the anchor, probably injured him. What was he going to do at that point, throw a paintbrush at us?"

"You sound just like a lawyer." I'd made her mad. "Just talk and talk about something you don't know anything about. When I was a kid I had to work the register in my parents' grocery store. There was a gun under the counter, and everyone knew it was there. It helped keep bad things from happening."

"You ever shoot it?"

"Not in the store, not at anybody. But my brothers would shoot it. They would go in after my father closed up, take the gun out and use their own bullets. Afterwards they'd clean it and put it back. He never knew the difference. That's how I learned to shoot; my brothers taught me."

"And you would have shot at that guy?"

"Did you know how many of them were out there? You're such a wuss. What if someone had started shooting at you? And I didn't shoot anyone, anyway, did I?"

She had a point, but I couldn't forget the image of her standing on the foredeck holding the enormous pistol. The recollection was persistent, dreamlike. What was strange about it? Maybe the expression on her face.

I said "Maybe you'll get another chance if he comes back."

She shook her head. "Please don't make fun of me, Tom. Anyway, he's never coming back here. We'll never see him again."

Out in the channel boats were slowing as they passed, to view the damage. A floating crowd of gawkers was growing. These were the folks who will drive halfway across town to cruise slowly through the worst earthquake-damaged neighborhoods. I called the haul-out yard and reserved a work slip. In a week we would go there for repairs.

81

13

As the memory of our arrests returned, I realized I had overlooked the obvious the night before. The most important thing Maria and I needed was a lawyer. Years ago, during an extremely relaxed phase in my life, when I smoked a lot of marijuana and wore my hair long, I remember being at a party and telling somebody I was a lawyer. His response was 'Man, you look like you need a lawyer.' Today I needed a lawyer. I called Leland Brown, at his office in Century City. He was the lawyer I always said I would call if I ever got in trouble. I had handled criminal cases for years but I didn't work the deep end of the pool. I sent the rapists, bank robbers and homicides to Lee. Also the coke cases when the weight got over a few ounces. Lee had the exact qualities you would want in a heavy hitter criminal defense lawyer; smart, completely fearless, and resolutely cheerful. He was calm under all circumstances. It has been said that his grandfather was the iceberg that sank the Titanic. Catholic schools had produced in Lee one of the few genuinely well-educated people I have encountered in the legal profession. When the Jesuits get through with you, you can go a hundred thousand miles between tune-ups, and argue any proposition with a straight face, no matter how improbable. I once heard Lee attempt to convince a Judge in Beverly Hills Municipal Court that it was not illegal to urinate in public. And that was in Beverly Hills, where it's probably illegal to urinate anywhere.

Lee laughed a lot when he heard what the problem was, but he agreed to put our Preliminary Hearing date on his calendar.

"I'll probably ask for a continuance though," he said. "No sense rushing into things."

That made sense to me. The continuance is to the criminal lawyer what the toilet plunger is to the plumber, except in reverse. It's an ever-handy tool that clogs things up. Delay almost always helps the defendant. Given enough time, witnesses forget, wander away, die, lose interest. Prosecutors leave their jobs, get married, go on vacations, get stuck with other cases, overlook deadlines. There are a thousand things that can go wrong, and a defendant only needs one. Criminal prosecutions don't age well.

"The only thing," I said, "is there any possible conflict of interest? You know, Maria was doing the shooting."

"Oh, you mean maybe we could argue that she shot at the whale and you were just sitting there fishing? Or better, maybe you were begging her not to shoot?"

"Actually, we were working as a team. I was lining in the shark and she was in charge of the .357. Anyway, if anyone has to take a fall, I'll do it."

"Very gallant of you. It'll be interesting to see how people react to a lawyer fishing for sharks with a .357. Why don't you just stay on board your boat at the dock and drink beer, like everyone else in Marina del Rey?"

"I do that too."

"Look, don't even appear at the Prelim. I'll show up and tell them I'm too busy to do anything until Fall sometime. If you're not there they can't proceed anyway. I'll get the bond exonerated and get you both OR'd.

This was vintage Leland Brown. If any other lawyer dared to try that, the Magistrate would revoke bail and issue bench warrants. Judges liked to do Leland favors. By the time the case was called for trial the Environmental Lady would probably be in Timbuktu helping the lepers, or defending harp seals from hunters on the Greenland ice. I started to feel better,

It was late afternoon and a mist was beginning to blow in off Santa Monica Bay. Maria had just returned a call from her supervisor to her mother's home in San Gabriel, which was where she lived as far as the County was concerned. She was suspended without pay 'pending the resolution of criminal charges,' Despite having the strongest union on Earth, L.A. County employees could apparently be suspended if charged with a felony.

After she hung up, Maria said a number of nasty-sounding things in Spanish, to no one in particular, and went down to the galley to cook. It was one of her major ways of coping with tension. I felt gloomy. I called my office and learned that our arrests had been covered by mid-day TV news. One of my best business clients had called and left word that he would no longer be needing my services. An address was left to which I was instructed to send his files.

In the galley Maria was blending a big chunk of Roquefort cheese with a quarter-pound of butter. Next to her on the counter was linguini, a heap of fresh lemon zest and several dried stalks of rosemary. These were the basic ingredients of a dish called Midnight Pasta. The spectacle of Maria's cooking always cheered me up.

By the time I got to the office it was late afternoon. I decided to ignore a thick bundle of telephone messages on the receptionist's desk and a stack of unopened mail. I once read that the first indication that a lawyer has gone off the rails is that he stops opening his mail. Maybe I don't take practicing law seriously enough. If I get a few bucks ahead, I tend to wander away, maybe fire up *Den Mother* and take a boat ride to somewhere. I think my attention span is too short, and getting shorter. Most of my classmates in law school seemed to live in the law library, and I have little doubt that some of them will die there. I intend to avoid this fate; the law library part, that is.

I was thinking about Franco Mandelbrot. If I could get him in a corner, would he tell his daughter to back off? He had given his daughter and son-in-law a beach house in Malibu. She didn't work, and Victor held a traditionally low-paying job as a County prosecutor. How much influence did the old man have?

I checked the address of the beach house in the phone book and called a title company I used to do business with. In an hour I had a faxed copy of a title summary. As I suspected, Mandelbrot was no King Lear; he was still the owner of the wedding present he had 'given' to his daughter and son-in-law. It was a good sign.

While I was still in the mood for research I called the Department of Regional Planning and spoke to a frankly hostile clerk, who took down the tract number I had copied off the bullet-ridden subdivision sign in the Santa Monica Mountains. It turned out that there had been an archaeological survey done on the project, as I had anticipated. The survey was a public document but copies were only available over the counter at the Hall of Records, downtown. I filled out a routing slip for my Attorney Service and marked it "rush". I would have a copy by tomorrow afternoon.

I checked in on my bag of bones; still in the back of the filing cabinet, together with the shopping bag of papers. Pearls from Señor Salas, the dumpster diver.

There was one item in my mail that I took the time to read. At my request I had been sent a pamphlet from the Native American Heritage Commission, an agency of the State of California. It was entitled 'A Professional Guide for The Preservation And Protection Of Native American Human Remains And Associated Grave Goods.' I particularly liked the sound of the phrase 'grave goods,' mingling, as it did, the notions of death and commerce. The instructions provided were clear and direct:

WHAT TO DO: The following actions must be taken immediately upon the discovery of human remains:

Stop immediately and contact the County Coroner.

The Coroner has two working days to examine human remains after being notified by the responsible person. If the remains are Native American, the Coroner has 24 hours to notify the Native American Heritage Commission.

The Native American Heritage Commission will immediately notify the person it believes to be the most likely descendant of the deceased Native American.

The most likely descendant has 24 hours to make recommendations to the owner, or representative, for the treatment or disposition, with proper dignity, of the human remains and grave goods.

If the descendant does not make recommendations within 24 hours the owner shall re-inter the remains in an area of the property secure from further disturbance, or: If the owner does not accept the descendant's recommendations, the owner or the descendent may request mediation by the Native American Heritage Commission.

If there were ancient Indian graves on Mandelbrot's subdivision, it was easy to see why he might have gathered up the bones and removed them. The alternative would have been a long leisurely minuet with the Native American Heritage Commission and a host of 'most likely descendants.' This perky but nonsensical phrase fascinated me, and it was interesting that the third time it appeared on the 'What To Do' list, 'most likely' had disappeared, and the phrase became 'the descendant.' Either way I could see it would be a tough call for Mandelbrot. In the present climate of political correctness, Native Americans were a hot ticket. Real estate developers were still the modern equivalent of the black-hatted villains of silent movies who tied pretty young girls to railroad tracks. Add to this the demographics of the Malibu area; socially conscious show business types, leftover hippies in all stages of consciousness, and just plain rich folks, whose reaction to all development was NIMBY; Not In My Back Yard.

A sleepless night playing boat games with the Harbor Patrol finally caught up with me. I returned a few calls, poked at my mail and left, taking with me the greasy shopping bag of papers I had purchased from Señor Salas.

14

I had been thinking it was about time to talk to Hersh and Murray, but the next morning they came to me, cruising up C basin in the flagship of the Sea Pioneers fleet: a classic 1939 Elco sedan cruiser, to which some ignoramus had later added a pre-fab fiberglass flybridge. Hersh sat up topside at the controls, wearing a large white captain's hat. His gold braid epaulets gleamed in the sun. On either side of the deck house was a wide blue and white banner bearing the legend

DONATE YOUR BOAT TO THE
SOUTHERN CALIFORNIA SEA PIONEERS

Two loudspeakers on the foredeck belted out the 'Sailors Hornpipe' at high volume and, best of all, standing in the aft cockpit was Murray Markoff in a sailor suit; a blue sailor suit with a pinafore blouse and a little white cocked hat. Very Gilbert and Sullivan. Murray had a serious look, as did his boss, and both would from time to time return salutations from passing boaters with solemn salutes. I noticed Hersh saluted with his left hand. As always, there was not a Sea Pioneer in sight. Hersh pulled the Elco into an empty slip on my dock. I got aboard, and we went for a little harbor cruise.

The three of us sat up in the flybridge as Hersh guided us down C Basin toward the Main Channel. I told them what I had learned about Rayburn, including the offer Larry had made to me over deep fried catfish at Chinois on Main and the fact that Maria and I had been arrested, which didn't seem to impress either of them.

Hersh said, "You're telling me we're being investigated for a crime that didn't take place?"

It was funny how the two of them reacted. Murray had the street-smart attitude that all authority is corrupt. He was amused at the idea that the Feds had the local Police chasing their own tails over Rayburn. A high-class confidence man such as Hersh, on the other hand, expects that everyone will play by the rules but him. The U.S. Department of Justice wasn't supposed to be running a con; that was Hersh's job.

"If he's not dead, Tom, just find him," he said. "Somebody must know where he is."

Murray said, "You want to find Rayburn, guys, it's easy. There's not many doctors hang out with Vic Cannizzarro and Lou Gizzi. The schmuck, he's got their pictures hanging in his office like they were movie stars. Y'imagine? Crooks he puts up on the wall." He shook his head. "I spotted those two goons first thing I walked in his office. I know friends of theirs, so when that cop started coming around I asked a few people if they knew what happened to Rayburn. The noise I got is that someone had a contract out on him, then the carjacker took care of him so they called it off."

I said "Why would anyone want to kill Doctor Rayburn?"

Murray said "I'm telling you, Italians were gonna hit him." He paused. "What I heard, the Doctor was a star fucker. He got kicks hanging out with crooks; don't ask me. In restaurants and stuff. You know, people look over and you're right there with the Godfather, shoveling up the mozzarella marinara. Then the guys figure if he can do surgery on your ass, he can do surgery on your face. And the schmuck always wanted to be a plastic surgeon. So if someone's on the lam, they would get Rayburn to do a little surgery on him, so he won't look like his wanted poster. And Doctor gets to practice where people can show off his work. I mean, how often is somebody gonna say 'you wanna see the beautiful job Doctor Rayburn did on my asshole?' He thought for a moment. "Maybe queer guys, I guess, but this way he's doing faces, and he loves it. Then he fucks up big time on some heavy hitter from out of town, the kind of guy you don't even want to know his phone number."

I said, "You mean some mafioso would kill Rayburn because he didn't like the results of his plastic surgery?"

Murray paused to salute a wedding party on the foredeck of a passing charter boat.

"Partly," he continued, "but the way I heard it they figured only Rayburn could make the guy, the way he looked after the operation, and he told them he was gonna have trouble with the IRS, so they wanted to shut him up before maybe he made a deal."

"But," Hersh said, "what about finding him? You said it would be easy."

"Well, kinda. What I do is I ask a friend of mine to take me to Vic or Lou and I ask them, if I do them a favor would they do me one back, and then I tell them Rayburn's alive and the Feds got him. Now you gotta figure they really want to whack the guy if they hear that, and all I want is, before they do it, they do something like take his picture holding the morning paper, so you can tell he was alive after the carjacking deal went down. And they give me the picture. That's the favor."

Hersh nodded approvingly. I didn't like it.

I said, "We should help set the poor guy up to be killed by hoodlums who didn't like their nose jobs?"

Murray shrugged. "You're the lawyer. If it's illegal then I won't do it. But I don't like it, being accused of killing a guy who isn't even dead."

I said "You'd feel better about it if he was really dead?"

The *'Sailor's Hornpipe'* concluded, and after a pause started again. They must have had it on a tape loop. I didn't feel like helping hoodlums murder Doctor Rayburn. I was considering the first rule of legal ethics, which is that when it starts to look like somebody may go to jail, make sure it's the client and not you.

I had had quite a long course of dealing with Lou Gizzi when I had been with the U.S. Attorney's office. Lou had been a confidential informant, except that none of the things he told us were about Italians. He was a calm, mild-mannered man, with strong features, dark hair and an athletic build, who liked to wear a golf shirt and a white cardigan, slacks and tassel loafers. He looked like someone you might meet at a country club, except for a heavy gold bracelet he always wore with the word 'Lou' spelled out in diamonds. He also used the word "cocksucker" a lot. Basically, he tattled to us on his enemies, and it was my job to meet with him to get whatever hot news he would have for law enforcement.

Lou's office was any branch of Benny's Always Open, a popular LA coffeeshop-style restaurant chain that was open twenty-four hours a day. Lou would call me, and I would check out a car from the motor pool and drive to whatever Benny's Lou was using that day. It was at one of these meetings that he proposed to me that we go into business together. He would give me the name and telephone number of somebody who was up to something, then I would call and tell this person that the U.S. Attorney's Office was investigating him. Then Lou would call and tell him that for a certain sum, Lou could fix McGuire. Lou told me we could split the money and, he said, we'd 'come up smelling like bandits.' I think he meant to say, 'come up smelling like a rose.'

After I left my job and set up in private practice, Lou

91

dropped by my office unannounced to see if I could be recruited in some way. It didn't bother him to learn that I wasn't interested in working for him. Very little upset Lou. On the way out he turned in the doorway of my office and said, "You know the difference between me and you, Tommy? You try to collect money with a piece of paper. When I go to collect money I bring a piece of pipe."

Cannizzarro and Gizzi were not the kind of people I wanted to get involved with. All those 'z's in their names reminded me of the sound of a dentist's drill. I tried explaining to Murray that I didn't want him to use his connections with organized crime to find Doctor Rayburn, particularly if it meant someone would realize he wasn't dead, and that the contract that had been put out on him was still worth money.

Murray looked disappointed. "It doesn't matter," he said. "If Rayburn's in the witness protection program they'll find out sooner or later."

I said, "What do you mean, they'll find out?"

"There's people who say they've got the program wired. They call it the witness destruction program. I guess they've got somebody inside."

Hoodlums in the Justice Department. Something we haven't seen since the Nixon administration. Maybe Larry Hayden would like to know about this, but I was out of the business of doing Larry favors. It sure made Doctor Rayburn's position sound risky, though. What if somebody killed him before I could prove he was alive?

We turned the corner on the Main Channel and started up C Basin again. I could see a cluster of boats up ahead, adjacent to *Den Mother* 's endtie, probably boaters admiring the vandalism committed on my hull. When we got closer I saw that a Harbor Patrol boat was conducting some sort of a recovery from the water. As we watched, the Harbies hauled up a limp body in a black wetsuit; clearly a deceased person. I thought I could see traces of red paint here and there on the neoprene surface of the wetsuit. The humainiac had returned, in a manner of speaking, to the scene of the crime. Since I was the one who had dropped an anchor on him and probably caused his transformation from vandal to fish food, I thought it better to keep silent.

It turned out later that the deceased had a broken shoulder and red paint on his wetsuit and was officially determined to be the person who had painted "whale killer" on my hull. No criticism was expressed of my role in the matter, which made for an interesting comparison with the fact that I had been arrested twice for supposedly shooting at a whale, not even for hitting one, just for shooting. Here was an actual human being as dead as Kelsey's cow. Lucky for me he wasn't a sea otter.

15

It was eleven thirty and I was on board, asleep, dreaming I was back on the redwood deck with the redhead. Maria was in San Gabriel for her brother's birthday, a celebration that had been going on for days and showed no signs of stopping. At that moment someone on the FBI dock started up his offshore racer, and I awoke. Offshore speedboats have big-block twin power and no mufflers to speak of. If the boat is close by and its exhausts are pointing toward you, the sound has a fierce snarly quality that evokes genetically encoded prehistoric fears. So I wasn't just awake, I was startled, and there was no question of getting back to sleep soon.

I padded up to the salon and looked outside. The offshore racer gnashed its rods and pistons in the night. There was a man wandering around on my dock, his body language suggesting to me that he didn't know where he was going. This was cause for concern. Things had been vanishing off the dock in recent years, most notably a fifteen horsepower outboard, the kicker motor off my little fishing boat. I wanted to discourage this kind of conduct. Also, your odd drunk would sometimes drift out of a nearby bar at closing time, and come down to the water looking for a cockpit cover to crawl under prior to passing out. More conduct I liked to discourage. So I opened the dockside salon hatch and stepped out on the dock. As I approached, the wandering figure turned toward me and I was astonished to see Larry Hayden in a rumpled blue and white jogging suit and serious sport shoes, looking very ass-over-teakettle, wide-eyed and needing a brush and comb. A shave, too. He spoke before I could say a word.

"We lost him, Tom. Rayburn's gone."

"Dead?"

"No, *gone.*"

Just like that. No apologies. No explanations. Before, he was supposed to be dead. Now he's alive but 'gone.'

I said "What do you mean, you lost him?"

"I can't tell you. We need to know if he contacts you or Markoff. We want to make sure you don't get involved in an obstruction of justice."

This was altogether too much for me. The man couldn't decide whether to plead or threaten.

"Larry, please, you're standing on my dock in the middle of the night and you're threatening me? Get a grip. Your people filed charges against me and I'm represented by counsel. Technically you've got no business even talking to me."

He looked so miserable I didn't have the heart to browbeat him much more, and I was curious as hell to find out what he had to say.

"Do you want to come on board? You got this far."

He nodded. We walked up the dock toward *Den Mother.* Larry truly looked like he had fallen off a building. He looked away from me as he spoke.

"I know I've treated you like shit, ok? It wasn't my idea. We have to talk, and I couldn't do it over the phone."

95

We settled down in the salon. Larry wanted coffee but I gave him Macallan instead. Nobody should drink coffee so late at night. He drank his scotch and told me that Doctor Rayburn was nowhere to be found, that he had vanished from the job they had got for him as a paramedic in a 'medium-sized American city,' which somehow put Larry's ass on the line. I wanted to ask him what effect this would have on Radovich's murder investigation. If Rayburn turned out to be gone for good, would the US Marshal's Service take the heat and admit it, or would they stick to the carjacking story? Larry could do a u-turn on me again and deny telling me anything. What also occupied my mind was what Murray had told me about Gizzi and Cannizzarro and the leaky witness protection program. I let Larry drink another inch of the Macallan before I spoke.

"This isn't the first time you've lost a federally protected witness, is it?"

Somebody turned off the offshore racer. Complete silence. From far away, a duck quacked.

Larry said "I can't discuss it with you."

"The way I hear it, there are foxes in your henhouse."

Larry carefully studied the scotch in the bottom of his glass.

I said "I'm not against trying to help you, even if you did have me arrested. You're lucky it's me and not Maria. Right now she wouldn't piss on you if you were on fire." What was I going to do to help him? I couldn't imagine.

Larry had a 'don't hit me' expression that I found embarrassing.

"But I want something back for it." No response. I figured at this point I could have had one of his kidneys.

I said "Your whole career's on the line, right?" He nodded. "Just call off the local heat on my clients. It's not fair to get the cops all stirred up over nothing. Be reasonable; Detective Radovich thinks there was a murder committed. That's what you wanted him to think. That's what you wanted everybody to think. There was a real dead body. Why? Couldn't you just have him drop out of sight, like a normal protected witness?"

He said "Because they would have kept on looking for him."

Whiskey had done its work on Larry. I now understood what had happened.

"No," I said, "it's not that they would have kept looking for him, was it? They would have found him. Because the bad guys have somebody inside the Program."

Larry was busy looking out the salon hatch at C Basin. I think he realized he had said too much.

I said "Can't you just tell the detective what he needs to know? And while you're at it could you please call off the whales? You don't really believe Maria and I shot at whales, do you?"

He finished his scotch and I sloshed him another good one. Chemical warfare.

"We're trying to fix the local police," he said, "but the whale stuff is coming out of D.C. from prosecutors right out of law school, new hires. We give them harmless stuff like marine mammals to practice on. They live in artsy little apartments on Capitol Hill and think they're saving the world." He paused to sip scotch. "Please, Tom, just work with me. I do witness protection full time now, OK? It's driving me crazy, the problems I have keeping track of them, keeping them out of trouble, keeping them happy. They're not a high class bunch. It's hard to find things for them to do, keep them from returning to a life of crime. I've got someone with a twenty-year career as an embezzler and forger, with three felony convictions. Now I give him a nice clean new life, and a clean record, and he wants to go to work in a bank. What am I supposed to do? Of course he wants to work in a bank. It's a homing instinct."

He looked intently at the whiskey in his glass, as if tiny battleships were carrying out a miniature naval engagement on its surface.

"If I don't find the Doctor," he said, "I might as well kill myself."

"Isn't that a little extreme?"

97

"If I don't, someone else will do it for me. Look, the Rayburn carjacking was my idea. It sounded like a perfect way to get him under cover without raising suspicions. I had no idea your clients were going to get investigated for it. I didn't know IRS had a hard-on for Rayburn, or about the boat-donation thing."

"So why not tell Radovich about it so he can stop investigating?"

"I did tell him. He wanted to hear it from Rayburn." His voice started to rise. "He wasn't sure maybe the Government killed him and I was trying to cover it up. He wanted to know who was DOA at the V.A. Hospital in Westwood if it wasn't Rayburn. Maybe we killed *that* guy. And when I go to get Rayburn to show him to the goddamn Detective he isn't mother-fucking there."

He was shouting now, standing in the middle of the salon waving his glass, which fortunately he had emptied a second time.

"Sit down, Larry. It makes me nervous to look up at you dancing around."

Larry sighed and seemed to get smaller. He sat, looking like he was about to cry.

"Now that we lost Rayburn people in Washington think I'm up to something," he continued. "They want to know why so many of my protected witnesses die or disappear. They're right, people are gone. Lots of them."

This went on for some time; bouts of recrimination and despair interspersed with onslaughts of scotch whiskey. I didn't learn much more; quite a few 'protected' witnesses had vanished from their new lives and some senior people in the Justice Department were beginning to worry that the program had been penetrated by the opposition. This of course I knew already.

As he went on, Larry become harder and harder to understand, as if he was speaking English as a second language. He kept repeating something that sounded like 'wazzin myfaw.' It reminded me of a meeting I had once had with a client from Argentina; a man with an Italian surname whose first language had been Spanish. He spoke English with an Italian accent, and all through our meeting, in which I paid him his share of a personal injury settlement, he kept saying 'tenzalla, tenzalla,' with the accent on the last syllable. After a while I decided he was invoking the Deity, as they say in the Middle East, *insh'allah*, God willing. So I started saying it too; 'tenzalla,' when it seemed appropriate. My client didn't seem to mind, and the last I saw of him he walked down the hall to the elevator, turned back to me and said "tenzalla." I replied "tenzalla." The elevator doors closed, and he was gone. Two weeks later I woke up in the middle of the night and realized the man had been saying 'thanks a lot.'

Larry finally passed out on the sofa in the salon. When I woke the next morning he was gone. I was mildly hung over. Both my utility bottle and my reserve bottle of Macallan were empty. Tenzalla, Larry.

16

I had in my hands a document entitled 'A Cultural Resources Investigation Of Three Hundred Acres Located In The Malibu Area of Los Angeles County, California;' Mandelbrot's clean bill of health. Apparently, Chumash Indians inhabited the Southern California Coast as long as four thousand years ago, and settled in many sites in and around what is now Malibu, but not on Mandelbrot's subdivision. The report stated that 'no significant cultural resources were discovered in the course of this investigation, and no isolated artifacts were found.' I also had a copy of the application Mandelbrot had filed for a permit to do the grading I had noticed when I visited the site, and here things got a little more interesting.

If you intend to disturb the soil in an archaeologically sensitive area like Malibu, State law requires you to hire a 'Native American Monitor,' whose job is to watch other people work and to stop the process if buried artifacts turn up.

According to the documents, Mandelbrot had hired Anthony Tenuta to be his Native American Monitor. I had represented a man named Tony Tenuta some years back. He was a cabdriver who had eased into dealing cocaine, which accounted for his nickname 'Tootie.' After some people in law enforcement got seriously angry at him, he eased back into driving a cab again, on probation this time. I hadn't spoken to him in a long time, but I pulled his closed file, got his number and left a message on his machine, which got me a return call the next day.

'Waddiya mean, do I remember you? You're my man, Tommy."

"Thanks. It's nice to be appreciated."

"What's not to appreciate? I walked for two kilos like Jesus walked on water. Every day I thank you."

"Still driving a cab?"

"Naw, it's too much for a guy my age. I got a better gig. I'm an Indian now."

"An Indian?"

"Actually, I'm a Native American. I said Indian 'cause I didn't want to confuse you. Some people don't know what it means, Native American."

"But Tootie, you're Italian."

"You wanna hear what happened? Remember my sister Ruthie, she came down and made my bail the first time?" I remembered her; a short, heavy lady with a bandanna. "Ruthie married a real Indian, I mean Native American, Howard Running Bear." He laughed. "I call him Streaker. He doesn't know what I'm talking about. Anyway, Howard is Chief of the Malibu Band of the Chumash Nation. That's what he calls it. And he's totally wired with County Regional Planning and the City of L.A. They make you get Native American Monitors for a lot of the construction, and if you want one you gotta come to Howard. He's got a lock on it, up to his ass in business, and then they started up the City of Malibu, and all of a sudden if you want to do construction in Malibu you can't fart unless you hire a Native American Monitor to stand there and sniff around. So

Howard's going nuts, he can't get enough bodies and he tells me, 'Tootie, you're in the family, get certified as a Native American and I'll put you to work'."

"It's that easy?"

"Naw, it's not easy. You've gotta have connections. Back in Yonkers where Howard was born his uncle is the Registrar, you know, the guy that takes care of the birth and death records?"

"Oh."

"Get the idea? I'm a full-blooded Chumash Indian, Tommy, and I'm driving a new Lexus instead of a cab. I'm telling you, it's the tits."

"So you know how to be a construction monitor? You have to be able to recognize when the bulldozer turns up bones or artifacts?"

"Yeah. It's not all fun and games. But so far in a year and a half I've done twenty-two projects; nobody's ever found nothing. Mostly, I get to stand around outdoors. I let my hair grow so now I've got a ponytail. I've got a nice Indian shirt I wear, and some jewelry, you know, silver and stuff. It looks good with my tan. So I hang around and drink beer. Tecate. All us Native American Monitors drink Tecate. It's sort of like our official beer, or something."

"So you get paid and you don't actually do anything?"

"I thought about that, 'cause some of the construction guys don't like it. You know, they're driving bulldozers and stuff and I'm just standing there getting paid more. But I decided it's like when I was a kid in New Jersey and my friend's father was a Rabbi? He got paid to sit in the corner where this kosher catering service had its kitchen and read the Bible. That way all the food was kosher. You gonna tell me that man didn't do any work? You gonna tell the Jews that ate from that caterer the food's not kosher, the Rabbi didn't do nothin'?"

"Tootie, calm down. I think it's wonderful. Listen, maybe you remember a project in Malibu. Up the hill from Big Rock, about three hundred acres with an ocean view?

"Yeah, just some grading, for a subdivision, right?"

102

"That's the one. Do you remember if any artifacts turned up?"

"I told you, Tommy, in a year and a half I never found nothing. It's embarrassing. The other Monitors laugh at me cause I never find nothing. I'm not Tootie no more. You know what they call me on the job? Ray. For Ray Charles."

17

There was still a law office to run. Mail arrived with remorseless regularity. Not long ago it had brought the legal equivalent of a letter bomb; a notice of a totally useless and stupid court appearance in an accident claim; the kind of case I tell myself I'm going to stop taking, but never do. I had teased this wretched paper out of its extra-long 'legal' envelope, and reflected that the most useless court appearances always took place at the most outlying courthouses. According to the Notice of Motion, I had been summoned to Superior Court in Anaheim, far to the South. A foreign country to a West Side waterfront type like myself.

Personal injury lawyers work on their cases as needed and get paid only if they win. Insurance defense attorneys get paid by insurance companies and work on their cases as much as they possibly can, since they are paid by the hour. I pictured my adversaries in the accident cases as swollen ticks, securely clamped to the sweet flowing breast of this or that insurance company. Their clients had such inspiring names; Equitable, Fidelity, Prudential. True, sometimes I envied their security, but who wants to be a tick? Besides, any insurance defense lawyer will tell you, you've got to take the insurance company's claims manager to lunch. I doubt I could manage it.

The Motion sought a Court Order compelling my client to remember how much time she had lost from work on account of her accident. When she had said 'I don't remember' in her deposition, opposing counsel had taken the position that she 'should' be able to remember; really, that she did remember and was refusing to testify about it. After she had testified that she didn't remember, I had instructed her not to answer further questions on the subject. Rather that sending a subpoena for her employment records, which were apparently going to be hard to get, counsel was now seeking an Order compelling my client to answer further; in effect, to remember. It would be a small spark of fun in a dull morning to watch defense counsel tell the Judge how to fashion an Order Compelling Recollection.

So I was southbound on the San Diego Freeway at 6:45 in the morning, prepared to perform the act that constitutes ninety-five percent of the practice of law; showing up on time, at the appropriate courtroom, in suit and tie, shoes shined, and in possession of the case file. 'Suit up and show up.' It's what we do. Once we get there we will utter profundities and wave our arms in the air. It's a living.

I had taken the former Richard Nixon Freeway, now renamed the Marina Freeway, from Marina del Rey, and had gotten about a mile south on the San Diego Freeway when my car started to burp and shudder, then slowed down. I headed for the center divider as the motor died, and coasted to a stop in the breakdown lane. To my right, all five lanes of southbound traffic were already thickening up. I sat there wishing I had a cup of coffee. After a moment, I was pleased to see a brown Lincoln Town Car pulling in behind me. A rescuer.

105

As I watched through my rear-view mirror I realized the car contained the Z's. Yep, Lou Gizzi and Vic Cannizzarro sat side by side in the front seat, Vic at the wheel. The two of them doing the gangster lean and sporting broad shit-eating grins. I wondered how this was going to sound to the Judge down in Anaheim: 'Hoodlums made my car stop on the freeway, and that's why I'm late, Your Honor.' Then Vic got in the front seat with me. Lou got in back.

Of the two, Vic was definitely the heavy, clad in a costly burgundy velour workout suit with white piping, his bulky frame reflecting a lifetime of traditional Italian cooking. He had a very nice haircut but a crabby expression. He smelled like cigars. Stuck in middle management in his fifties, he was never going to become Don, or Capo, or whatever they called it now. In my rear-view mirror, Lou still looked like an amiable golf pro, in the familiar white cardigan sweater. He noticed me looking at him and smiled pleasantly. Between the two of them, Lou was the man in charge. Then a small, dark, gnome-like person I hadn't noticed got out of the Lincoln, popped my hood and did something to my car.

Vic said "start it up, kid," and I did. After a little cranking it worked just fine. He continued, "Don't make a problem, ok?" He reached in his pocket and pulled out an audiotape cassette, which he inserted in my dashboard tape deck. I expected something dramatic, a desperate ransom plea from Doctor Rayburn, or some such Godfatherish stuff. Instead the familiar sounds of Mozart's Symphony in G Minor, the 'Jupiter,' filled my car. Vic smiled. The gnome drove off in the Lincoln.

"I love Mose," Vic said. "It's beautiful, izznit? Learning about this stuff is part of a program I'm doin', 'cause I never got no education when I was a kid. Now I'm learnin' to listen to Mose. I'm developin' sulfa steam. You know what I'm talkin' about?"

I nodded. I was familiar with the problem. Vic turned up the volume a little and adjusted the bass.

"It's not just music," Vic continued, "I'm learning how

106

to cook. Don't laugh." Like I was going to laugh.

From the backseat Lou said "You should see this guy in the kitchen. Last night he cooked for four of us. *Zuppa Di Vongole*, then *Conchiglie E Animelle*. My mother couldn't have made it better."

Vic smiled a goofy smile. "All my life since I left home I've been eatin' outta cans, or else in some cheap-ass joint, you know what I mean? Part of developin' sulfa steam, you ask yourself what would make you feel good if you knew how to do it. So I been takin' lessons from a real Italian chef."

I said "What is that *Conchiglie?*

"Scallops and... I only know how to say it in Italian."

Lou said "Sweetbreads. Scallops and sweetbreads." Then he said "We got a problem with a friend of yours, kiddo. Drive the car."

The cooking segment of my kidnapping was over. I found a gap and pulled into traffic. Lou said "take us down to the Giant Doughnut," and Vic directed me into the far right-hand lane, down to the Manchester off-ramp, then off to the right and into the parking lot of a doughnut stand that featured a four-story-high doughnut on the roof, a spectacular creation of what appeared to be chicken wire and spray-on concrete, painted brown. On its side was lettered the words 'GIANT DO-NUT.' Inside my car the first movement of the 'Jupiter' symphony was finishing up. Culturally, it clashed with the doughnut.

"You've sure been in the papers a lot," Lou said. "Shooting up whales. That stuff's gotta be illegal."

Clearly, I was in the midst of my allotted fifteen minutes of fame.

"Yeah," I said, "it is illegal, but I didn't do it."

"No kidding," Vic said. There was admiration in his voice. "You got the right idea, Tommy. Don't cop to it, no matter what."

I thought about the long American tradition of the Heartwarming Hoodlum, from *Guys and Dolls* through *West Side Story* to *The Sopranos*. Nice, undereducated guys with your basic Sam Goldwyn approach to the language. They

107

only commit crimes because they had bad childhoods. It wasn't their fault, and for better or worse we learned to love them. The problem with this domestication of violence is that, inevitably, the chickens will come home to roost.

Lou said "We're looking for somebody."

I said "In my car?"

He ignored me. "Doctor Rayburn. Guy does assholes."

"I saw it on TV." I said. "Someone shot him."

From the backseat Vic snorted. "Yeah. We been hearing the Boy Scouts shot him, and you represent them. Believe that shit? When's the last time the Boy Scouts shot anyone?"

I said "Didn't the Boy Scouts shoot Bambi's mother?" He scowled at me. Oh, well.

Lou said "The cops like that bunco guy for it, your client."

How did they know this? "I can't talk about it. It's privileged information."

Another snort from the backseat. "He can't talk about it." A mocking falsetto, carrying the strong suggestion that my preference in the matter might not be respected.

Lou said "Where's Rayburn?"

I said "He's dead. I saw it on TV.

Vic said "If you're keepin' this guy it's gonna be unhealthy."

I said "I'm keeping a dead guy?"

Vic said "Don't fuck with me."

It was time I asserted myself. "Look, are you guys kidnapping me, or what?"

Vic laughed and turned to look at Lou in the back seat. "He thinks we're kidnapping him." He turned back toward me. "Some people got no appreciation. We bail you out when your car breaks down, play you a nice tape, classical, then we take you out for coffee and doughnuts. And you're complainin'?" He turned back to Lou. "You want a jelly-filled with the coffee?"

Lou wanted a jelly-filled. I didn't want anything.

Vic got out of the car and walked across the parking

lot toward the 'DO-NUT.' At that moment I had an inspiration. "Lou," I said, "I think I want a cup of tea. Let me go tell him."

As I had anticipated, Lou was too savvy to let this happen. Instead, he removed the ignition key, got out of the car and walked in the direction Vic had taken. Every car I have ever owned has had a spare key I keep in the dashboard ashtray. I gave Lou a minute, then started up the car and drove back to the freeway. This was definitely going to be a blow to Lou's sulfa steam. Mine, however, was in great shape.

At intervals on the way down to Santa Ana I found myself thinking about *Conchiglie E Animelle* and hoping that I never had to eat any.

18

In warm weather, *Den Mother* tended to establish a colony of fruit flies in the galley. They were quick and hard to catch, but I found them vulnerable to being sucked into my twelve-volt hand-held vacuum cleaner. Not only was this an efficient way of getting rid of the fruit flies, but Maria said it satisfied my hunting instinct, which all men possess. It's true, I did feel good about it.

She was laughing at me as I stood in the galley inspecting the transparent front section of the Mini-Vac, which contained at least a dozen doomed fruit flies, walking around in dazed confusion. I remembered the classic gag: 'time flies like an arrow; fruit flies like a banana.'

"What do you suppose they want?" said Maria.

"I don't think they want anything in the way you and I use the word. They're just flies. They eat, they breed, lay eggs, you know."

"I don't mean the flies, I mean the hoodlums at the

Giant Doughnut. What do they want?"

"You're assuming those goons exist at a higher level of intelligence than the fruit flies. That's far from clear."

I made a graceful thrust and pirouette and sucked up another fly.

"Maybe so, Tom. But you won't be able to suck those scuzzballs up with a vacuum cleaner." It was an entrancing thought. I imagined tiny little Gizzis and Cannizzarros, furiously banging on the inside of the Mini-Vac, demanding to be let out. Let them eat flies.

"You made them look stupid," she went on. "The next time you see them, they're going to have something more in mind for you than coffee and doughnuts."

"Like getting back the Mozart tape?"

"Do you want to be a smartass or do you want to try and solve the problem?"

"I can never decide. Anyway, they want Doctor Rayburn and I have no idea where he is. I'm not even sure if he's alive or dead."

The weird thing about the fruit flies was that they seemed to learn about the threat posed by the Mini-Vac. They got harder to catch from day to day, even from hour to hour. The day I started I could totally decimate them, but after a while the few survivors started to get wily and hard to suck up. This didn't make any sense, because there could be no communication between the flies inside the Mini-Vac and the flies that remained outside. So how could the survivors be learning?

Yesterday had not been a good day at the office. Detective Radovich had called with more questions for Murray and Hersh. Leland Brown's office had called to give Maria and me a new date for our Preliminary Hearing. Harry Hatcher had called from the *Times* with another request for an interview. *60 Minutes* had expressed interest in the whale story and Harry was in a feeding frenzy.

Maria said "What they want is Doctor Rayburn. The hoodlums, not the flies."

"If you can believe Murray, the Mob has a direct line

111

into the Witness Protection Program. Murray told me sooner or later they find out where all the witnesses are."

Maria laughed. "They're all informers, aren't they? Sneaks? They should expect to be betrayed. After they're finished helping the Government put their friends in jail, who really cares about them?"

"Well, they're supposed to be protected, not slaughtered. That's what was driving Larry Hayden crazy when he was here the other night."

"Drinking up all the whiskey?"

"Drinking up all the whiskey. He'd lost control of his witnesses. He told me witness protection was all he did these days, and now he can't find some of them, or at least he can't find Doctor Rayburn."

Maria said "So now nobody knows where he is."

"Right. Tell that to Gizzi and Cannizzarro."

I had caught all the fruit flies. I plugged up the snout of the Mini-Vac with a paper napkin to keep the captured flies from crawling back out, and replaced the unit on its charger. It was Saturday, and Maria and I had gone fooding. This had involved a stop at the Farmer's Market, on Fairfax, then north to Little Russia, the neighborhood around Fairfax and Santa Monica Boulevard, where we scored a pound of bright reddish-orange salmon roe, imported from Russia; crisp, dry and not too salty. With this, you could stoke a caviar habit without vast personal wealth. Let others dream of Rolls Royces. If I ever make it big I intend to eat a lot of Beluga. Maria and I would often spend a day hunting and gathering in this way; voyages I referred to as 'Touring Los Angeles Down The Alimentary Canal.'

So as the light faded and damp settled down on the Marina we prepared and ate salmon roe on toast points made from seedless rye bread purchased at the Farmer's Market and garnished with *crème fraiche*, chopped onion and parsley. Also included was a salad and a bottle of white Bordeaux.

As I spooned leftover salmon roe into its plastic container I reflected that Gizzi and Cannizzaro were not necessarily where I should be focusing. I finished putting away the remains of dinner, then cleared the largest possible space in the salon and spread out a plastic dropcloth. I put on a pair of bright pink rubber dishwashing gloves and carefully laid out the contents of Rigoberto Salas' shopping bag of trash, lately removed from the Balducci's dumpster.

I've heard this activity referred to as Garbology. As the name suggests, there's a science to it. First you collect and throw away the useless stuff, like empty tin cans and food wrappers, cereal boxes and paper towels. Fortunately this ecologically sensitive household must have separated its trash; there were no newspapers or glass bottles, and no plastic. There were cigar butts, Q-tips, cotton balls, tissues and similar household trash. Once I got started Maria withdrew to the galley where she remained with a glass of wine and a new police procedural. Finally, I was left with bills for subscriptions to the *New Yorker*, and something called *Back Pain Magazine*, a bill for $1,250 from a company in downtown LA called Museum Pieces, and a statement of charges from a phone bill, showing long distance and local toll calls. I saved the bills and the phone statement and threw the rest away.

19

I had no difficulty making an appointment with Franco Mandelbrot on the premise that my client was interested in his Malibu subdivision. The local real estate market was on its ass and he probably didn't have much to do. He agreed to meet me at his club, Sylvan Glade, in Topanga Canyon. Leland Brown had cautioned me against this. I always tell my criminal clients just what he told me; stay away from everyone involved with the case, don't visit the crime scene, and so on. But lawyers make lousy clients, and the bag of bones was an irresistible temptation to me, the kind of poker hand that you just have to play. The compulsion to stay in the game and see what happened was driving me up Pacific Coast Highway on a beautiful Sunday morning.

At Topanga Canyon Boulevard, I turned right, and started to gain altitude. After years of drought, Southern California had recently experienced its wettest winter on record, and Topanga Canyon was lush with vegetation. I had never heard of a health club in Topanga Canyon, but I followed Mandelbrot's directions up Topanga Canyon Boulevard and past the bridge at Topanga Center. A few miles further on I realized where I was going. Sylvan Glade would have to be a new name for Sunny Acre, the well-known nudist resort that had been a center of controversy in the Topanga area for years. I recalled the scene on the redwood deck; this was a family that liked to take off its clothes. What Mandelbrot had evidently planned for me was a mixture of Topanga chic and winning through intimidation; a business meeting in the buff. I glanced over at my attaché case, in which I had stashed a nice-looking femur from my collection of old bones. The morning was not developing as I had planned.

I followed a dirt road past a sign that said 'Private - Keep Out.' Sylvan Glade was not encouraging walk-in trade. After a mile of dirt road I drove through an open gate and parked next to a broad hilly lawn crowded with naked sunbathers. If you think the human body is inspiring, stay away from social nudism. Gravity, the great enemy of physical beauty, had done its work at Sylvan Glade.

Hardly anyone glanced my way as I walked over to the office through a group of naked picnickers. I was wearing tan slacks, cordovan loafers, a white polo shirt and a blue blazer, and carrying my leather attaché case. I felt really silly; major industrial-strength silly. Inside the office three pleasant middle-aged clothed ladies worked behind desks. Mandelbrot had left word with them and they were expecting me. Mr. Mandelbrot, I was told, was up at the pool. I could undress in the locker room next door if I wanted to, but nudity was optional at Sylvan Glade. I think that without the attaché case I might have decided to go native, just to prove to Mandelbrot that I wasn't afraid to do it, but I couldn't deal with the image of myself naked with an attaché case.

I left the office and walked up the hill toward the pool. I definitely preferred my clothes and my illusions to the reality of collapsing flesh visible all around me. After such knowledge, what forgiveness? To my left down the hill, a

115

volleyball game was in progress. Why are nudists compelled to play volleyball?

It was easy to tell which one was Mandelbrot. Amidst a crowd of swimmers and sunbathers, a small, bald, intense-looking man sat next to the pool at a metal table supporting a beach umbrella. Somewhere in his sixties, with a deep, unfashionable, rich-folks tan. He was pecking at a laptop computer open in front of him on the table, and as I approached he picked up a cell phone and started pecking at it instead. On his wrist was the largest gold Rolex watch I had ever seen. A real horse-choker. Technically, I suppose you could say he was naked, expect he was mostly covered with curly gray hair from neck to knees; a little bald gray weasel. He motioned me over to his table and I sat and waited for him to get off the phone. I suddenly realized how stupid this was, that I had no idea what I was going to say to him about my nonexistent client, or how I was hoping to get from Mandelbrot and his sub-division to the prosecution for shooting whales, and the fact that it depended on his daughter's testimony.

Being surrounded by a profusion of sagging bums and boobies did nothing for my composure. At that moment he put down his cell phone and turned toward me.

"You are obviously Mr. McGuire."

It was time to do something really tricky, so I decided on instant candor.

"Mr. Mandelbrot, I have something I have to tell you. I don't have a client interested in your land. I just said that as a pretext to meet with you."

His expression didn't change. "I know that," he said. "I know who you are, too. You're the poor sap my Katie has been feeding on this season. You're the whale guy, right?"

I nodded. He smiled a little weasel smile. His bright blue eyes were set oddly in his head, and seemed to be looking in two different directions. A naked Marty Feldman.

"Before it was whales," he went on, "it was dolphins. The surfers were annoying them, according to Katie. She had investigators from Fish and Game down to the house for

116

weeks. The surfers wouldn't come near us. Some of the neighbors were a little pissed off with her for swimming naked, too. I don't know what their problem was; she's a good-looking girl."

He smiled another vaguely demented smile and shifted on his chair. His genitals were barely visible in a thicket of gray pubic hair. They looked like small pink animals crouched under a bush to avoid a predatory bird.

At that moment his cell phone rang, or squealed, in the way that they do, and he began a conversation with someone about sewer easements. I sat back and focused my attentions on a trio of pubescent girls at poolside. After a while they wandered off. By the time Mandelbrot put down the phone my fantasies would have been good for an easy three to five in the Pen, and I had shifted my attention to some of the resident mastodons to drive evil thoughts from my mind.

"You like the view?" he said, smiling at me.

"There are certain aspects of life that are wasted on teenage boys," I replied.

"Like teenage girls?"

"Yep."

"Some things," he said, "it's better to dream about them then actually try to do them. Take me, for instance, I'm old enough to be somebody's grandfather, if my daughter would ever calm down enough to do something normal like have a family."

"She doesn't want kids?"

"She doesn't need kids. She's got whales, dolphins, harp seals, foxes. Did you know the foxes are threatened down at the Ballona Wetlands, near the Marina? It's a big bruhaha, if you listen to Katie. I've got friends who are going to develop the whole area. My daughter and her crew are going to stick those foxes right up somebody's ass."

"That's going to hurt."

"Hurt?" His voice rose. "It's going to cost someone a fortune. With a little bad luck it could kill the project. And you know the funny thing? I've given her everything she

117

needs. Her and that cockamamie husband of hers, the lawyer. When she got married I built them a house at the beach. She makes a good living from investments I made so she wouldn't have to live on her husband's pathetic little salary. All the money came from real estate development. It's what I do. But you should hear her talk about my business. To her a real estate developer is scum, slime. Like it says in the Bible, 'how sharper than a serpent's tooth it is to have a thankless child."

"Actually, that's Shakespeare."

"Huh?"

"King Lear, I think."

"What's the difference? When we started grading up in Malibu she didn't have a civil word to say to me for weeks. All she could talk about were the coyotes and rabbits, and the Indians. Would you believe it? They've been dead for centuries, she's worrying about Indians. We're alive. Why not worry about us?"

Something clicked in my mind. I had assumed the bones in the bag had been collected up the hill and brought down to the beach. Maybe I had it backwards and I had intercepted the bones on their way up, not down. In that case it would have been the daughter, not the father, who was responsible. Nobody puts Indian relics on his own subdivision. I opened my attaché case and took out the femur.

"Have you ever seen anything like this before?" I asked.

His expression clouded. He gave the bone a long look. Then he took it from me and examined it carefully, turning it over and over in his hands. His eyes rose to meet mine. They no longer appeared to look in two different directions.

"Why did you bring this to me?" he said.

His mood had definitely changed for the worse. I thought of several possible answers to his question but couldn't think of a good one. "I think it came from your property," I said. Actually, it had come from the back of his little blue truck, but I didn't want to say that.

118

Mandelbrot was building up a head of steam, but controlling it. Now he was an angry gray weasel. I wished I could rewind to when the femur was still concealed in the attaché case. That's what life needs; reverse. Or at least fast forward.

"Do you know what this is?" He was making an effort to control himself.

"It's a femur, I think. An old one," I replied.

"No, no, I don't mean that. Do you know where this came from?" Somebody's leg, I thought, but he answered his own question. "It's a museum piece. It came from a museum. Look."

He was pretty excited by now. He held the bone up and rotated it slightly. Near one end, in tiny black letters, someone had written a code number: 'E-0667MOW.'

"If this bone came from my property," he said, "it's because somebody put it there."

Now he was gesturing with the femur and poking it at me in a semi-threatening way. Without thinking about it I grabbed the other end. It was a moment that evoked the dawn of the human race, a furry little naked man about to assault me with a leg bone. So I held on tight to my end, he did the same, and for a moment we struggled in silence. Then we started to attract some attention from the other sunbathers, some of whom raised their heads from their lounge chairs to look at us, like big pink sea lions disturbed on a beach. I let go of the femur. I think Mandelbrot was embarrassed. I know I was. I had not noticed the little numbers written on the bone.

I said "Look, somebody found this bone in a little blue truck with 'Mandelbrot Development' written on the side."

"Katie drives it. It's hers." He didn't sound surprised.

"Maybe I could help you figure this out," I said, "but I need your help too. Your daughter is going to put me and my friend in prison for something that never happened."

He sighed. "You're only the latest problem. I told you. Katie and me..." He trailed off. "...it was better when she had a mother."

119

"I'm sorry. What happened?"

"Oh, I divorced her. She moved out of state." He looked thoughtful, then said "Look, Mister...I'm sorry I forget your name...I don't think you've got a problem anymore. I think Kate's had a change of heart."

I waited, hoping he would say more. The subject seemed to be closed. The young girls I had been watching returned to the pool and began playing a game in the water, throwing a ball back and forth.

Mandelbrot said "You can be my guest here for the day. Why not stick around, take your clothes off, get some sun and exercise?"

"I'm not sure that would be a good idea."

I didn't feel like being naked in public, at least not there, at Sylvan Glade, among the nymphets and the mastodons. I wanted to go home, but where was my damned femur? I didn't see it anywhere.

20

I never found the femur, but I had plenty more bones, and that night I spread them out in the salon. Maria and I examined each one. They all had numbers and letters in black ink, similar to the code number on the femur.

"You don't suppose," I said, "that ancient Indians did this to make the skeletons easy to reassemble?"

Maria ignored me. "It's what Mandelbrot said. They're all from a museum. This is environmental sabotage. If you bury these bones on a construction site and someone digs them up, they have to stop the project."

I heard a noise on the dock and looked through the salon hatch. Bobby Baxter was standing there holding Captain, the little white dog. Bobby had a glazed look, and was probably halfway through a bottle of scotch or can of Spar varnish, whichever it was. Bobby said "Do you know a boat called Filthy Fish?"

"Never heard of it," I replied.

"I was playing with my marine radio and left it open on channel sixteen. There's some guy calling Den Mother from a boat called Filthy Fish.

I thanked Bobby and went up the ladder to the bridge and turned on my radio. It wasn't *Filthy Fish* but Bobby was close.

"Den Mother, Den Mother, Den Mother. This is the vessel Gefilte Fish, Kilo Charlie Foxtrot Five Niner Zero Eight, calling the vessel Den Mother. Come in."

It sounded like Murray Markoff, the only person I knew who had a boat called *Gefilte Fish.*

"Vessel calling Den Mother, this is Den Mother, call sign Whiskey Romeo November Seven One One Five. Switch and answer on Channel Six Eight, Channel Six Eight."

"Roger, Den Mother, Switching to Six Eight."

"Den Mother this is Gefilte Fish on Six Eight, over."

"This is Den Mother, over."

"Den Mother, this is Hymie on Gefilte Fish."

Murray's father had been named Hymie. I knew this because Murray had become incensed with Jesse Jackson's use of the term 'Hymietown' as an anti-Semitic slur on New York City. "What is that asshole talking about," Murray would say. "My father was named Hymie." So I knew it was Murray and I knew he wanted to keep his name off the air.

"Hymie, good to hear from you. Where are you, over."

"I'm out in the water, in Lombardia. I'm all the way down the dirt road, as far as you can get from the bar, over."

So Murray was in Cat Harbor. It takes some explaining. Catalina Island is private property, with the exception of one square mile at the East End, which is the town of Avalon, and a leasehold at the West End, known as Twin Harbors, which includes Isthmus Cove on the mainland-facing side of the Island, and Cat Harbor on the seaward side. The lease was once owned by the Lombard family, and some of us had taken to calling the place Lombardia. There are commercial facilities on the Isthmus Cove side, including boat moorings, a grocery store, gas dock, restaurant and bar. Cat Harbor is at the end of a dirt road about a half-mile from Isthmus Cove. There's no commercial development on the Cat Harbor side. If you pick up a mooring there, it's a long walk to the bar. So, Murray was in Cat Harbor.

"Roger, Gefilte Fish. What are you doing there? Over."

"I've got the *tuchis maven* with me. He was visiting with me and then things got outta hand all of a sudden, people showing up. We had to get out, and this seemed like a good place, over."

Maria stood at the bottom of the ladder leading up to the bridge, looking puzzled. She didn't understand.

I said "It's Murray. He's got Doctor Rayburn on board."

"He does?"

"Sure. The proctologist, right?" She nodded. "The *tuchis maven*, that means rear-end expert in Yiddish. It's him."

Maria said "What's this all about?"

"Everybody's looking for Doctor Rayburn, and it sounds like he turned up at Murray's boat."

She gestured down the dock. "Murray's boat is right down there, in its slip."

I keyed the microphone to transmit. "Hymie, I read you. I've got your location and crew. What do you need? Over."

"Everything, pal, everything. We don't feel like going to town, and we could use groceries, drinking water, a fresh twelve-volt battery, some money, some scotch, anything else you can think of, over."

I looked down into the salon. Maria didn't seem pleased at the prospect of an immediate, unplanned trip to the Island. Personally, I never need much of an excuse to go for a boat ride, but this one was a dandy.

"Gefilte Fish, I'll see you tomorrow. How will I identify your vessel? Over."

"Listen up..."

Murray's sense of pitch may have left something to be desired, but he was obviously attempting to whistle the 'Sailor's Hornpipe.' So Murray was on the Elco they had

124

given me a ride on the other day, which made sense because Murray's liveaboard boat, the real *Gefilte Fish*, was a rambling wreck and couldn't have left the dock safely, let alone taken him across the channel to Catalina.

"Roger, Gefilte Fish.   Understood. I'll see you soon. Over and out."

21

By the time we got it together and cleared the breakwater it was 11 a.m. and there was a serious onshore breeze. Swells were three to four feet from the northwest and seemed to be building, along with a vigorous chop. Our compass heading put us broadside to the swells, for maximum roll, while the chop would smack against the starboard bow and spray the front glass at the bridge. Bumpy and messy. At least the sun was shining.

As a form of entertainment, traveling in powerboats is vastly overrated. For one thing, powerboats are noisy. They often smell of engine exhaust if the wind is wrong, and there is apt to be a great deal of bucking and plunging around in all but the flattest seas. For every perfect voyage you can expect three or four more when many objects inside the boat wind up on the deck broken, and spilled beer, or worse, sloshes in the scuppers.

Liveaboards have more possessions on their boats

than recreational boaters and it takes a while to put everything down before leaving port. Over time, things that are going to self-destruct at sea do so, leaving their more hardy or stable brethren intact. You instinctively tend not to buy fragile stuff. Sometimes an object that has been well-behaved for years in a wide variety of sea conditions will decide that today is the day, and become airborne with no discernable provocation. After years of driving the boat with the TV shock-corded to the top of a cabinet in the salon, the cabinet and TV went over together, in a patch of bumpy water off Ribbon Rock on the back side of Catalina. Made a noise like doomsday but didn't hurt the TV or the cabinet. Shook up the Captain and crew pretty good.

Twenty minutes out of the breakwater, clanking and banging noises from the galley told me we hadn't done an adequate job of stowing gear for sea conditions, so Maria went below and chased down the noises. After a few minutes she returned, and sat beside me at the helm. Dolphins were leaping out of the water all around us, pacing our progress through the water.

"Tom," she said, "do we have any ammunition?"

With more than two hundred gallons of gasoline on board, one did not often think of firearms. Maria probably had her Smith & Wesson .357 Magnum and I had an old Italian Mannlicher-Carcano bolt-action rifle, the kind that Lee Harvey Oswald was supposed to have used to kill President Kennedy. One look at this antique would make a conspiracy buff out of anyone, but it fired an impressive-looking boat-tailed fully metal jacketed slug that was designed to pierce armor. I had bought it at a garage sale after reading an article in a yachting magazine about modern-day pirates off the West Coast of South America.

"Why do we need ammunition?" I said.

She frowned. "It's a simple question," she said. "Do we have any?"

"Mostly we've got .38 caliber snake loads for the .357, and a couple of boxes of rounds for the Carcano. They don't make them any more. If we use them up we'll have to get reloads. Oh, and we're out of cannonballs. We used them up sinking that Spanish man-o-war off of Pacific Palisades last Sunday. What do you have in mind?"

A wry look. "Your head is a cannonball."

Maria looked over her shoulder. A huge yellow offshore racer was coming up behind us on the same heading, snarling in the penetrating, expensive way that they do.

"I'm trying to think ahead," she said. "Murray must be worried or he wouldn't have gone to all that trouble to conceal his location. You've got those gangsters mad at you and they're looking for Doctor Rayburn so they can kill him, if I'm understanding things. And your friend Larry Hayden is a slimebag, isn't he? And *he's* looking for Doctor Rayburn too. Put it all together, and I just wondered if we had any ammunition."

The offshore racer had pulled ahead of us and was disappearing in the mist. The dolphins had vanished, and we were completely alone on the water. It was about mid-channel, with very limited visibility. Just us, thundering along at thirteen knots. Sometimes this is an exquisite pleasure. Sometimes it's creepy. Today it was a little of both.

Maria said "Murray went out to the Island because he was scared, didn't he?"

"That was my impression. He wants to protect Doctor Rayburn."

"Okay, so my point is, if there should be any rough stuff, wouldn't you like to confront it with something more impressive than your weenie in your hand?"

"Some would say..."

"In your dreams."

"...it's a formidable weapon." A delicate pause. "Okay," I said, "weapons you want, weapons you got," and I told her where to find our meager arsenal. "Bring it all up to the bridge and let's sort it out."

I got on my cellphone and called my office. I never get tired of this trick. These are the toys I wished I had when I was a little boy; two-way radio telephones, real guns, powerboats. I've called friends on the East Coast from out in

128

the water, just so I could say "you'll never guess where I'm calling from." You have to call someone in Manhattan this way in the middle of Winter. Let the bastards suffer.

*   *   *

   It's really Catalina Harbor, and the high point of land adjacent to the entrance is Catalina Head, but they've been called Cat Harbor and Cat Head so long I think most people have forgotten. Cat Harbor is a long narrow finger of water surrounded by rolling hills that rise up to steep cliffs on the west side, at Cat Head. I've never seen more than a dozen boats in the entire place at one time, although there are moorings for many more.   The place is so calm and unspoiled, it's sometimes unsettling for a city boy like me, and it reminds me of the story of the guy from New York who went camping and found that he couldn't sleep without the sound of breaking glass.
   The mouth of the Harbor is flanked by Cat Head on the West, and a semi-submerged obstacle, Pin Rock, on the East. The back side of Catalina is completely exposed to the open ocean, and if you come up from the West End when there's a big swell running, the opening in the cliffs doesn't show until you are close to the area of breaking waves just offshore. Once you're that close, it would be difficult to turn a boat like *Den Mother* around without broaching to in a trough and possibly capsizing.   So you hope, as you steer your boat straight at the cliffs, into the surf, that your GPS is working correctly and they haven't moved the harbor since the last time you were there.
   As we drew forward into protected water I could see the Elco moored in front of an old pier on the west side of the harbor. There was a figure in a loud shirt in the aft cockpit, waving at us. If you run a nineteen-forties era Chris-Craft, people know your boat. Try that with a plastic Uniflite.
   We picked up a mooring next to the Elco and went over in the inflatable to see Murray. He was lying in a lounge chair in the aft cockpit, drinking beer and watching

129

something on a miniature twelve-volt TV. He wore a crumpled straw hat and was barefoot. His shirt displayed a tasteful motif of parrots and pineapples. I couldn't tell whether he was scowling at me or the TV, but he still managed to look like a race track tout who had retired to become a beachcomber. He was watching a golf tournament on the tiny TV.

"What's the point," I said, "you can't even see the ball."

He turned slowly and regarded the two of us standing on his swimstep.

"That's not what it's about," he said. "TV is just a noise. I don't think people look at the picture much anymore. Only like when it's nine eleven or Monica Lewinsky or some other disaster you don't wanna believe happened, then you look at the picture."

"You're running a TV," I said, "no wonder the batteries are low."

Murray grinned. "I knew you were comin', and we couldn't start the engines anyway, so what's the difference? We're outta ice too, so the beer's warm. Otherwise I'd offer you one. You know, when the batteries are low this TV picture gets even smaller. Doesn't hurt the sound any."

Maria looked impatient. She had been the one to go get Murray's extremely heavy new battery.

"Maybe when you put in the new battery," she said, "the golf tournament will be over. This is the only battery you're going to get from me."

"No problem," said Murray. "We could get all we want from the store at Isthmus, but the Doctor says he saw familiar faces on the patio in front of the bar, so we don't go there."

"Where is the Doctor?" I said.

He was clearly not on board. We all turned and looked over at the shoreline. In front of the pier there was a bright yellow inflatable raft pulled up on the beach, well above the water's edge. Murray got up and walked across the deck to the TV. The picture had shrunk to the size of a cigarette pack. He turned it off.

"He went for a walk," he said. "Maybe someone should go find him."

The wind whistled over the low, grassy hills. *Den Mother* bobbed placidly at the adjacent mooring. I wondered what it would take to put me into this world completely, without the need of returning to what most people would call real life. Catalina does that to me.

"I'll go over to Isthmus and look around," I said. "But tell me something, where did Rayburn come from?"

Murray said "You mean like, where do babies come from?" He walked back to his lounge chair and popped a beer, which must have been warm because it foamed over his hand and onto the cockpit sole.

"Excitement like this I don't need at my age," he said. "He tries to call me on the boat a couple times, I'm not there. Then he shows up one night, lookin' like a street person. Clothes on his back, that's it. He tells me they parked him as a paramedic in some ambulance service they run in Dallas. Some kinda temporary deal because they're in a hurry, Rayburn's gotta disappear quick and they don't have time to do the complete number, make a whole new I.D for him, so they use a loaner, or whatever, a spot they keep ready for emergencies. So they take him to Dallas, what does he know? The schmuck, he's fifty-five years old and they've got him jumpin' in and out of ambulances, pickin' up O.D. junkies and all kinda gobbitsch off the street. So one night they get a call, somebody's passed out, and when they put the guy in the ambulance his friend wants to go with him to the hospital. Once they get rolling they find out the whole thing's bogus; the passed-out guy wakes up and the two of them turn out to be hoodlums, spaghetti heads, they're gonna hijack the ambulance and take Rayburn back to Los Angeles. Pretty slick, huh? Two weeks it took them to find out where he was and make a move. What kinda halfass witness protection is that?"

Maria and I looked at each other, remembering Murray's revelations and Larry Hayden's complaints; somebody had an inside line on the 'protected' witnesses.

The irony was that both sides, Government and Mafia, had an equal interest in keeping the secret; the Witness Protection Program was a roach motel; they check in, but never check out. And yet, from the Government's perspective, after the witnesses had been persuaded to testify, what difference did it make what happened to them? As long as the secret never got out, everything was fine. But it would be wrong.

"So how did Rayburn manage to turn up at your boat?" I asked.

"The two palookas in the ambulance tied up the driver and wanted to turn off the siren and flashing lights, but they didn't know how. While they were fucking around with it, Rayburn jumped out the back and ran. He had just enough dough to get a Greyhound back to Santa Monica."

Maria laughed. "I'll bet those two got spanked for that when they got home."

The day had turned cold, and she was bundled up in something ratty she had found in the cabin.

Murray shrugged. "Whatever. That was the week I started to get popular. Before Rayburn shows up I start getting phone messages from some schmuck who said his name is Richfield, he wants to talk to me about a law enforcement matter. That's what this putz says on my machine, a law enforcement matter. Ya believe it? Like it's *Dragnet*. Then my neighbor in the next slip tells me two big, well-dressed guys were on the dock looking for me. Well-dressed, you know they're not from the Government, so they're probably the muscle that rousted Rayburn in the ambulance, and they gotta be royally pissed 'cause they lost him. So I figure now they know where I live, sooner or later they'll be back, so when Rayburn shows up and fills me in, first thing the next morning we go for a boat ride. The Elco was all gassed up and ready. Hersh doesn't even know it's out of the barn." He looked at Maria as if seeing her for the first time. "You know," he said, "that's the jacket I loaned to Rayburn."

The same thought seemed to occur to all of us: where

was the Doctor? It was late in the day, the sun had gone down below the ridge to the west. I looked across the water to where the yellow inflatable was pulled up on the beach. The tide was coming in. In an hour or so, the raft would be adrift.

22

I was sitting in the dark, surrounded by throngs of seriously inebriated people dressed as pirates. Most of them were wearing some combination of a red bandanna headband, black eye-patch, a silly looking plastic cutlass, and most commonly, a black tee shirt with a skull and crossbones and the legend 'Buccaneer Days - Isthmus Cove - Catalina Island.' It was Buccaneer Days. Three or four times a year the management at Isthmus Cove sponsors a theme event; Halloween, Forth of July, Cinco de Mayo, or whatever else they can think of to encourage boaters to come over for the weekend. Whatever the theme, there are suitable costumes and gimmicks for sale at the store, as well as the inevitable tee shirt marking the occasion.

It's okay to drink at the Isthmus. It's like one of those turnouts on the Interstate where the sign says 'Rest Area," only here the sign would say 'Alcohol Area.' There are no cars, and drunken boating is handled on the basis of 'don't ask, don't tell.' Isthmus Cove is completely isolated. There are no overnight accommodations to speak of. When you want to crash, you go back to your boat, or lie down wherever you happen to be. There is a County Sheriff's station, but arresting someone for drunkenness at Isthmus Cove would be like rousting someone for loitering at an old folks home.

Tonight, a band was playing on the patio in front of the bar, where I was sitting surrounded by pirates. Country and Western. Was it supposed to be pirate music?

There are summertime evenings at Isthmus that are pure magic. The air is still and warm. Soft lights are mounted in the palm trees, and the boats bob peacefully at their moorings in the darkness just off the beach. Sometimes you can see mainland lights, but usually you can sit at the outdoor bar and imagine you are anywhere but Los Angeles; Tahiti, Pago Pago, Fiji. It probably helps that I have never been to any of those places, but the effect and the transformation can be intense, a powerful feeling of being in a tropical never-never land, with yachts.

This evening was not one of the romantic ones. For one thing, it was crowded. Although the Cove was dark, you could see that there were boats at almost all of the moorings. Inflatables and other dinghies were three deep at the dinghy dock. There were people everywhere, in and out of costume, in ragged clumps and crowds, and it was the kind of summer night in which people run around and hoot and shout with a kind of tense expectancy, just below hysteria. Some people were dancing to the Country music, in couples or alone, moving into patches of bright light under the palm trees, then back into darkness, onto the sandy beach. The wind had stopped blowing when the sun went down and I could smell the salt air, sometimes a little marijuana, rum, coconut oil suntan lotion. The tired-out strains of *'Okie from Muskogee'*, played loud, drifted over a kind of low roar from the crowd. Pirate music. In this moment you could do whatever you wanted to do.

135

What I wanted to do was find Doctor Rayburn. Considering the number of people who might have had similar intentions and who might also know my face, I had purchased and put on the obligatory bandanna, eye-patch and tee shirt. I drew the line at the plastic cutlass. I had brought a little digital flash camera along to take Rayburn's picture if I found him. Something to show Detective Radovich.

As I sat in front of the bar a dogfight broke out on the patio. A small white terrier was terrorizing a large black Labrador retriever, and I recognized first Captain, the Maltese, and then Bobby Baxter, his owner. Bobby was shirtless, revealing a large sunburned belly. He sported the kind of captain's hat for sale in marine supply stores everywhere. He wore plastic sandals and what may have been the last pair of madras Bermuda shorts currently in existence in America. He had a drink in his hand, and looked half in the bag. I called out to him, and he disengaged Captain from the Labrador and came over to sit beside me.

"It doesn't matter," he said, shaking his head, "they show up everywhere I go."

It was as if we had been interrupted in the middle of a conversation. I didn't know what Bobby was talking about, and told him so.

" Remember the marlin trip?" he said. "They're here. The same guys."

"The guys you went fishing with?"

"No. The guys with the machine guns. The Coast Guard drug guys. The sonsa bitches..."

Words seemed to fail him. He gestured vaguely out toward the moorings, then took a sip of his drink, put it down on the bench and gathered his little dog up in his arms. Captain looked alarmed. The clamor of the Buccaneer Days crowd was not to his liking, the nervous energy. Or maybe it was the Country and Western music.

I said "You're talking about the guys who boarded your boat out by San Miguel Island?"

"There's two of them sitting at the bar right now. Their

goddamn boat is out on E Row, E four or five. I picked up the mooring right in front of them, D four, and there they were behind me, staring at me like a tree full of owls."

"You think they recognized you?" I said.

"No. I don't know. I recognized them. And there's more guys in a speedboat, a big yellow Cigarette over at the gas dock."

We peered out into the shadows. The yellow offshore racer Maria and I had seen that morning was dimly visible at the end of the pier, next to the fuel pumps. Light was shining from its portholes, and there were people moving around in the cockpit.

"Are those guys Coast Guard too?" I asked, gesturing toward the Cigarette.

"They're guys in suits," Bobby said. "I don't know. But they were in a dinghy this afternoon, going back and forth to the other boat. They're together. Who comes to the Island in a suit?"

I had a pretty good idea who. Marine radio channel sixteen is monitored twenty-four hours a day by all kinds of people, and Murray's shenanigans with 'gefilte fish' and 'Hymie' had not worked. All they had to hear, it now occurred to me, were the words *Den Mother* on the radio as Murray tried to hail my boat. Big Brother had broken the code. They were probably at Avalon too, at the other end of the Island, looking for Rayburn.

I suggested to Bobby that Captain might need a walk, and we left our bench among the drunken buccaneers and strolled out the dock toward the gas pumps and the yellow Cigarette racer. Up close it was a lot bigger than it had looked from the helm of *Den Mother* that afternoon. Then, it had looked like a toy. Up close it looked more like fifty feet long. The cockpit was brightly lit and there were two people standing there looking up the dock at us. As we approached I heard the strains of Mozart's '*Magic Flute,*' and began to wonder if Bobby had been right about recognizing the Coast Guard.

"Bobby," I said, "this may turn out to be a problem.

137

Why don't you hang back here with the dog. If it looks like things are getting out of hand, call out as if you had just walked down here and recognized me, but don't get close unless I wave you over, Okay?"

He nodded, but looked puzzled. "Are they friends of yours?"

"No. Whoever they are, they're the opposite of friends."

"That's Mozart, right?" Bobby said.

"I'm afraid so."

We approached the Cigarette more closely, and as I had feared there were Gizzi and Cannizzarro, in suits, and leather shoes calculated to mar the fiberglass deck of their mighty offshore racer. Here at the Isthmus they looked seriously out of place, except for the predatory look taught to all hoodlums during basic training. Real pirates must have looked like that. To these guys, I realized, everyone was a potential victim. They were cats looking at the world through mouse-colored glasses. In a harbor full of make-believe pirates they were the real thing.

Vic caught my eye and nudged his buddy.

"Hey, look," he said, "it's fuckyknuckles."

Fuckyknuckles? Lou looked surprised but also a little flustered. He looked down belowdecks and seemed to be waving off someone who was coming up from the cabin, but his gesture evidently went unnoticed as Larry Hayden emerged from the interior of the speedboat, looking haggard in another dirty workout suit. Didn't this guy have any real clothing?

It was too good a moment to miss. As *'The Magic Flute'* played on I held up the camera I had taken along to gather evidence of a live Doctor Rayburn, and snapped a flash picture of the three surprised mariners. It was the wrong move. Vic jumped out on the dock and grabbed me by the arm, moving faster than I would have believed possible, and I was more or less thrown into the cockpit of the Cigarette. As Larry watched, the two of them hauled me to my feet and shoved me back against the transom. Vic picked up my camera from where it had fallen on the deck and tossed it

138

overboard.

"No pictures," he said. "What're you, *Life Magazine*?"

An answer did not seem to be required, and I offered none. An unused dockline was coiled on the top of the transom behind my back, and I was able to push it into the water without attracting attention. I was starting to wonder where Bobby was when I heard Captain's furious yapping and Bobby calling "Hey, hey, that's my friend you've got there." There were two or three other boats tied up at the fuel dock, with people on board, and a couple of weekend pirates on foot as well, and we were starting to attract attention.

Larry said "Let him go, fellas," and The Z's stepped back. Evidently Larry had them trained. "We thought we'd run into you here," Larry said to me, "but we didn't find your boat. You're in Cat Harbor, right?"

I nodded. My back hurt where it had hit the transom. Why was I being so damned cooperative?

Around us swelled a rich musical tapestry of Mozart and Bobby's barking dog. Bobby must have thought I was getting beaten up by the Coast Guard because he was shouting something about police brutality, which was driving Captain into a further frenzy. Lou walked across the cockpit to the control panel and turned the music up louder. More people were walking out on the dock to see what the noise was about. The Country band had stopped playing. We were now the only show in town.

Nobody seemed to be paying any attention to me so I stepped off the boat onto the dock. Larry was now at the helm of the Cigarette and suddenly Isthmus Cove swelled with the penetrating sound of the huge unmuffled engines. The boat was facing toward the beach, and to leave the dock it would be necessary to go into reverse. I had no doubt where Larry and his crew were going; right around the West End to Cat Harbor and *Den Mother*. A journey of seven miles or so which Would only take them a few minutes in the big yellow speedboat.

I watched as Larry throttled the engines down to idle, put them in reverse and backed away. He had just cleared the end of the dock when one of his propellers picked up the loose dockline I had shoved into the water. It was good strong line, half-inch nylon three-strand, with the bitter end securely cleated to the transom. When it wound up on the propeller and pulled tight one engine stalled.   When you wrap nylon rope on a propshaft it's almost impossible to remove underwater without exactly the right tools, which nobody is likely to have on board. Either way, no one was going anywhere in that vessel until they sorted things out. At least the cockpit lights and the sound system still worked. At the moment it was mostly Mozart.

23

I sprinted down the dirt road from Isthmus Cove back to Cat Harbor after escaping Larry and the Z's at the gas dock, leaving behind a confused Bobby Baxter and dog, and a gathering crowd of drunken pirates. I found Doctor Rayburn sitting at a picnic table by the dinghy dock on the Cat Harbor side, dressed in a strange assortment of outdoorsman's clothes. Just sitting there in the dark. The rising tide had evidently floated Murray's yellow inflatable off the beach, leaving the doctor stranded.

I took him back with me to *Den Mother*. Murray and Maria were on board. The battery we had brought out for Murray sat in the aft cockpit where I had left it. No effort had been made to get Murray's boat operational. Even on one engine I figured Larry and his buddies would be able to make it around the West End to Cat Harbor soon enough, so we fired up *Den Mother*, dropped the mooring and got out into the ocean.

Doctor Rayburn sat next to me in the bridge, watching me drive the boat. He told me he had left all his possessions behind in the escape from Dallas, except for the paramedic's uniform he was wearing, and fifty dollars in his pocket. The one charge account in his name that still worked had been with an upscale middle-western supplier of duck-hunting equipment, and he was wearing some unusual special-purpose clothing he had ordered; a pair of quilted down-filled pants, a rather comical long-billed duck hunter's hat, a complicated hunter's vest, and a pair of leather and rubber lace-up boots designed for slogging around in swamps looking for ducks. He looked grayer around the temples than I remembered him. He did not look like a doctor. Actually, in his duck hunting gear he reminded me of Elmer Fudd.

As I drove the boat Doctor Rayburn related to me his short unhappy career as a plastic surgeon.

I said "It's amazing to me that you could learn to do plastic surgery by taking a two hundred dollar seminar."

He frowned. "I know how to do surgery. Any doctor can do surgery. You don't need a special license to do plastic or reconstructive procedures. The seminar was just to learn a few special techniques."

He seemed hurt, as if I had doubted him, but as I learned, doubts about Doctor Rayburn's abilities as a plastic surgeon had become fairly widespread in certain circles.

"I never intended to actually do plastic surgery professionally," he continued. "It was a hobby of mine, something I was looking into. It has no application to proctology." This delivered totally deadpan.

"I never thought I'd get the opportunity to actually do any plastic surgery," he continued, "but my friends asked me to. Lou said it was important."

"Lou Gizzi?"

"That's right."

"I saw the picture on your office wall," I said. "How did you meet those guys?"

"The same way I met Murray Markoff, a hemorrhoidectomy."

143

"Lou's?"

"No, Victor Cannizzarro. A charming man. We shared a taste for fine food and wine, and he knew all the best places. Restaurants I had never heard of."

"I'll bet."

"It wasn't until much later that I found out they were famous."

Famous? I'm always annoyed when I encounter what I call the Jesse James syndrome; the veneration of criminals by people who ought to know better. Most criminals I had encountered were not worth admiring by anyone except other criminals.

"Sometimes," he went on, "when we were having dinner somewhere I would meet a friend of theirs who wanted plastic surgery and didn't seem to mind that I had a different specialty."

"When did you figure it out?"

"Oh, after a few procedures it was obvious that the goal was not so much to improve their appearance as to change it as much as possible. Chin implants, cheek implants, major rhinoplasty. They were all men with prominent features, big noses and ears. I made them all smaller. The noses and ears, I mean. I would tuck the ears in, and I did a lot of little turned up noses. Retroussé, you know?"

"What were you telling me about a pig nose?"

He pursed up his mouth a little and looked over at the instrument panel.

"One patient had that problem. After the last procedure his nostrils were apparent. Some people call it a pig nose. But it was worse than that. He had a saddle deformity, which means that the bridge of the nose collapsed. It happens sometimes. His nose curved down and then back up again, like a saddle. Think of Michael Jackson."

"Do I have to?"

"It is considered unaesthetic when you can look directly at a person and see into the nostrils," he said.

"There's a lot of intolerance around."

He looked at me sharply. The man was not overly burdened with a sense of humor and like all such people he distrusted it in others.

"It's a risk when you start with a prominent Roman nose," he said. "I told you, it can happen. It was unfortunate that it occurred together with the saddle deformity and the difficulty with the cheek implants."

"The cheek implants?"

"Oh, one of them slipped down, so that it was lower than the other. So we had three problems with one patient. He was very concerned."

"I can imagine."

"And he had been a handsome man, too," Rayburn continued. "Actually, he was extremely angry. He was not an educated person, and he was very abusive with me. He said his face looked like it had been run over by a truck. Really, he exaggerated, but the serious problems started when I showed him the photographs."

"What photographs?"

"All plastic surgeons take photographs of their patients. Not just before and after; you sometimes do studies of a particular feature, a nose for instance, to help you and the patient to decide what would be the best approach. I would also take pictures during a procedure and during the healing process. When word got out about the photographs, Lou told me my life was in danger. I couldn't understand it; it hadn't been a secret. I don't know what they thought I was doing with a camera if I wasn't taking pictures. At least when they were conscious, they should have realized. They would have killed me to get those photographs, Mr. Hayden said. Can you imagine that? When I found out the trouble I was in, I was also being audited, and my wife was divorcing me." He clutched my arm and looked around fearfully, as if he expected his ex-wife or a Mafia hit man to appear on the bridge of my boat. "It was a chance to solve all my problems at once, Tom. May I call you Tom?"

I had thought of Doctor Rayburn as a curiosity, an

odd species of butterfly, but now I felt sorry for him. He was on the edge bigtime, and had no prior experience at it. At this moment he had neither an old nor a new identity; sort of a soft-shelled crab, with something of the same potential to wind up as somebody's dinner.

He turned toward me and grinned. "The thing about being dead that I liked the most was the opportunity it gave me to screw my ex out of her support payments."

Suddenly I wanted to go home.

24

We had almost cleared the West End when I saw the yellow speedboat. Maria stood beside me at the wheel. I had sent Doctor Rayburn below, where I could hear him arguing with Murray about something. I was wondering how I had been so stupid as to put my passengers, my boat and myself at risk, floating around in an obscure place, and at night, to make it worse. I never like to go boating at night.

We squinted out into the gloom. The yellow Cigarette loomed about a hundred feet away, its hull broadside to us. I took the boat out of gear. Below decks, *Den Mother's* big Chryslers rumbled in neutral.

Maria said "What do we do now?"

She had loaded the Carcano and put it on the dashboard with the bolt drawn. I took some satisfaction from imagining what those big metal-jacketed boat-tailed slugs could do to the Cigarette, but it would be a case of mutually assured destruction. Both boats had large fuel tanks full of gasoline, not diesel. I assumed there were firearms on board the Cigarette; the Z's probably never went anywhere without a handgun or two, and my experience had been that most large boats had a rifle stowed in an equipment locker somewhere. Defense against the pirates that every boat owner prepared for and nobody ever saw, at least not in Southern California waters. Until tonight. If they shot at us at all, we would be likely to blow up, catch fire, and burn to the waterline. And we would probably have enough time to do the same to them. On the ocean side of Catalina, at night, assistance of any kind was out of the question. VHF radio transmission is line of sight, and the high cliffs behind us would block any signal from getting out to Isthmus Cove or the mainland. In the other direction was Japan. Same with cell phones; we were in a dead zone.

"That" - I gestured to the Carcano - "is not going to help. I'm not going to die fighting over a proctologist."

So we sat, both vessels drifting slowly on the broad swells. We were less than a mile offshore, which might have been in too close, except for the current, which was taking us toward the West and slightly away from the cliffs. No chop, no moon, haze beginning to thicken up. All our cabin lights were off. Nobody said a word.

I said "Can you see their transom?"

Maria picked up the binoculars and took a look.

"Yes. The right side outdrive is cranked up out of the water. What happened?"

"They wound a dockline up on the prop."

"How do you know that?"

"I'll tell you later.

"Okay. So what?"

"Right about now they're deciding to come alongside of us, tie up and come aboard."

"I saw a movie like that once."

I said *"Captain Blood*. It had Errol Flynn in it. Can you see Larry Hayden swinging through our rigging with a cutlass in his teeth?"

149

"We don't have that kind of rigging."

"No. But I'll bet whoever's driving that boat has never tried to do close maneuvers at night with power out on one side."

All boaters have experience putting their boat alongside a dock. It's the first thing you learn. It's very different when the dock is moving too, and doesn't want you to come alongside. And if you're used to twin power, close maneuvering on one engine takes some getting used to.

So the way it worked was, whenever they went forward their port-side engine would kick them to starboard. So they would make a tight turn to starboard and come up alongside us, and each time they tried that, just as they were about to come alongside, I would wait until the last moment and back away. It turned out they couldn't back up either, without kicking the stern off course and getting sideways to everything. They had a loud hailer, and used it. I have never heard anything intelligent uttered through a loud hailer.

After a few minutes of this Maria said "Whoever's driving that thing is getting seriously upset."

She was right. A rattled, insecure powerboat operator will use too much throttle, jerking the gearshift back and forth, trying to force the boat to do his bidding. Boats don't like this, and will respond by getting balky and stubborn. If you're at the helm you'll get to a point where your hands are shaking, your insides soaked with adrenaline, all confidence gone. I was scared enough, mostly of a collision, but I had the idea that my adversary at the controls of the Cigarette was close to being all used up.

That was when they started shooting. Two shots. Large caliber, by the sound. It focused my mind, and I heard the loud hailer guy say "channel nine." I turned the VHF radio on to channel nine and waited. Maria picked up the Carcano, shot the bolt and aimed it at the Cigarette.

"Er.... Tom?" It was Larry Hayden's voice.

I keyed the mike and said "Yes?"

"Uh, we got a problem." I could hear Lou Gizzi in the background, saying "tell that cocksucker..." something I didn't catch.

"Nothing like the one you're going to have if you shoot another round. I've got a crewmember here with a semi-automatic nine pointed right at you. sixteen in the magazine. You can have them all, if you want."

Lies, but I wasn't going to tell him our heavy firepower was a World War One bolt-action relic, was I? I tried to remember if I had ever fired the damn thing.

There was a moment of silence. Then a click as Larry came back on. "Who's the shooter, your girlfriend?"

Maria glanced at me. A nod, and she'd have opened fire. I shook my head. Only in the movies can you shoot your way out of things. Murray and Doctor Rayburn stood at the bottom of the ladder to the bridge, looking up at us like kittens that somebody might decide to drown. I said I wasn't going to die fighting over a proctologist, and I meant it. He wasn't even my proctologist. If he hadn't made that crack about screwing his ex-wife out of her spousal support I would have felt worse, but I felt bad enough.

"Doctor," I said. He looked away. He knew what was coming. "It looks like you may have to go back into the Witness Protection Program."

He said "They'll kill me."

I said "It's worse than that. You're dead already. You were dead on arrival at the Veteran's Administration hospital in West LA. You probably don't remember, 'cause you weren't there."

Doctor Rayburn said "Huh?" Then he said "Somebody should have thought this thing through." He looked at Murray as though it was his fault. "This isn't anything like what Mr. Hayden told me was going to happen."

It was almost funny.

At that moment the big yellow speedboat loomed off our starboard side. They had managed to get in very close, coming much too fast. A dark figure was standing on the foredeck of the Cigarette, a rope in his hand. I put the port-side engine into reverse and gave it a little gas, widening the gap between the two boats. Then they hit reverse while going much too fast in forward, blowing up the transmission. I could hear it go 'whump,' a several-thousand-dollar sound. Now they had no power on either side.

I turned off the VHF radio. I had a pretty good idea what was going to happen next. Slowly, the distance between us and the Cigarette increased. After ten minutes, we could no longer see them. I put my mighty Chryslers into forward, and slowly throttled up to twenty-five hundred rpm.

Maria said "Where are we going?"

I said "Home."

25

There is a hierarchy when it comes to courtrooms at the old Federal Building. Senior Judges get the grand high-ceiling ones on the first and second floors; the full-bore WPA cost-no-object churchlike chambers, lavishly paneled with mahogany and turgid thirties-style architectural brass. Every sound made in these temples of justice gets sucked up somewhere; silence piles up thick and deep. Magistrates have no such luck, especially junior Magistrates. Now they call them Magistrate Judges, but they have the same relationship to real Judges, at least in the Federal system, as nurses have to doctors. So if you're not too sick, a nurse can take care of it.

Our nurse today was Magistrate Judge Kaiser, who did not rate a full scale doom room. Magistrate Kaiser's courtroom looked more like a large secondhand furniture showroom, specializing in the kind of fat indestructible varnished oak office furniture which would never have come into existence on this planet were it not for the United States Government. If America ever suffered nuclear annihilation there would be nothing left afterwards but this furniture, maybe slightly singed, but usable, definitely usable. And use it we would, to start a new Government and make more courthouses to fill up with more indestructible oak furniture. There would be cockroaches also, I understand. After the bomb, that is.

Such were the thoughts which distracted me as Maria and I sat on the edge of this sea of varnished oak interspersed with spectators and unfortunates such as ourselves, the defendants. The air in the long low-ceilinged room was stale, and smelled of wax and despair. Lawyers and their clients drifted in little eddies around the spectator section, talking in low tones. As always in a criminal courtroom, fear was in the air.

It was true that I had once thought it was kind of funny, the business with the whales, but this had worn off awhile back, I think when we were arrested for the second time. I don't think the funny part had ever taken hold with Maria. She sat next to me with a frozen fuck-you expression of the type perfected by Latinas of the San Gabriel Valley, kind of a chrome-plated industrial-strength fuck you. She was wearing one of her work suits, the kind of suit worn by women who occupy middle management positions at the phone company; the kind that looks like a policeman's uniform without the brass buttons. She looked like she might need a can opener to get undressed. She wore black pumps and carried a large heavy black leather purse.

In front of all the indestructible chairs and tables was a low dais, on which Magistrate Judge Kaiser sat at a fat varnished oak lectern, and in front of this arrangement Leland Brown danced and smiled. He was wearing a blue striped seersucker suit with a red and white striped tie. I owned a similar suit and I suppose some other lawyers do too, but Lee was the only L.A. lawyer I knew who had the balls to actually wear the thing. Any fool can wear a seersucker suit in Boston; around here it takes nerve. And

155

with the tie; Betsy Ross eat your heart out.

Lee noticed us and winked in our direction. Lee was indestructibly cheerful. It was a great asset when, for example, he had to explain to a jury why the eighteen bullets his client had been forced to shoot into his girlfriend's husband in self defense had mostly entered his back. I had been in court with him that day.

"You know," Lee had told the jury with a broad smile, "when you shoot someone he spins around."

No such *sang froid* would be needed today, as it was only a Preliminary Hearing. Kindergarten stuff. First the Assistant U.S. Attorney puts on a minimum of evidence, then your lawyer makes a motion to dismiss which is denied, then the Magistrate sets a date for you to enter a plea before a real Judge. Then you can go home if you're not in custody or your bail doesn't get revoked. So if it was so cut and dried, I was thinking, why were we still there at eleven-thirty?

I had worked in courtrooms with Lee and could read all his little non-verbal stuff; shrugs, grimaces, an eyebrow up a bit, the roll of an eye, and it was clear something good was coming down. As the morning wore on Lee got happier and happier. The Assistant U.S. Attorney, an intense-looking young man with a florid brown moustache, a sincere but poorly-cut gray suit and scuffed wing-tip shoes, was projecting grim embarrassment.

Lee finally came back to where we were sitting.

"Is the complaining witness a redheaded dame with big tits?" he said. "The one who says she saw you in the boat?"

Maria looked suspiciously in my direction; I hadn't told her about the tits. I confirmed that such was indeed the Environmental Lady.

"Well," Lee went on, "they're all pissed because she's not here. They told her she had to come to Court to testify today and she was supposed to be eager to do it. They can't locate her and she was the only witness they were going to put on. Actually, she's their whole case. They can't go forward without her, and I'm not going to stipulate to a continuance if I can get away with it, except they continued this hearing three times because I asked them to, so it kind of makes me look like an asshole."

"What's the point, Lee," I said, "she'll testify sooner or later. She's dying to put us away."

Lee winked at me. "Funny you should say that. Can you keep a secret? Both of you?" We nodded. "She's dead." He couldn't have looked more satisfied if he had done it himself. "At least I think she is. The USA's office doesn't even know. I got a call at home last night from a buddy of mine in Homicide. They found her on some property her father owns up in the mountains, with a skeleton." A skeleton?

Maria was pissed. "How come you waited till now to tell us?" The purse twitched ominously at her side.

With a straight face Lee explained that he hadn't wanted to take the excitement out of the morning right away, and that he thought we would appreciate the news more after waiting two and a half hours in Court. And anyway what if his buddy at Homicide had been talking about someone else and the lady had appeared after all? He also claimed that if he had told the Prosecutor what he had learned about their complaining witness they would naturally have suspected that he, Leland Brown, had somehow been responsible. This wouldn't sound so dumb if you knew Lee. Nobody would ever actually suspect that he would murder the complaining witness in a case against his client, but amazingly lucky things tended to happen to Lee a lot, and you just had to wonder.

I didn't know whether to believe what Lee was telling us; he had been in and out of the courtroom a few times and could have been on the phone, but it was vintage Lee. I had seen him do things like this more than once. It was obvious Maria did not appreciate Lee's sense of fun. I wasn't sure if I did or not.

Lawyers and civilians see things differently. Maybe it was working in places like the US District Courthouse that bent the viewpoint. The metal detectors at the doors, for example. Two of them, actually, at each entrance; one for employees and another for the public. Employees could walk through with more metal, but the machine's sensitivity was turned way up where the public had to walk through. So who says the Federal Government isn't sensitive to the public? It had been necessary for me to remove my belt, because of the buckle, and ultimately to go through without my wallet. Credit cards, said the guard, who had chuckled and told me about the difficulties of a hotshot trial lawyer who finally had to go through without his shoes. Big metal buckles on his Ferrigamos. I wanted to ask him about a new non-metallic Glock nine-millimeter semi-automatic I had read about which was guaranteed to pass through the detectors undetected, but it had seemed needlessly provocative.

Ceilings in public areas of the Courthouse bulged with large plastic pods containing, I supposed, closed circuit cameras. The guards at the Main Street entrance had a bank of at least twenty small TV screens. What did they display? It had seemed rude to look, but after I had finished using the urinal in the first floor men's room, I looked up at a optical kind of gadget in the ceiling, smiled, and bowed. Big Brother is watching you pee. The Courthouse had always seemed menacing, but it had been a kind of menace based on the threat of what they, the Government and its minions, its Judges, could do to you, a defenseless citizen. Now there was another kind of threat, the legacy of nine eleven; there might be a common disaster here in which everyone would be fucked at once, Government, Judges, prosecutors, defendants, their lawyers, dogs, cats. It flickered just at the edge of perception, a sustained low pedal tone, a terrorist Mass in D Minor. And that, my chickens, is why lawyers like Leland Brown sometimes think it's funny to annoy people in tricky ways.

Finally Maria and I walked out into the sunlight, blinking and a little groggy, as if we had just sat through a double feature. Our case had not been heard. Lee had waived time.   We would be back in two weeks. What would you call this movie?

26

It turned out parts of Leland Brown's story were true and parts of it weren't. Kate's husband, Victor Balducci, had discovered her body at the site of her father's subdivision in Malibu. The cause of death was blunt force trauma to the head. There was no actual skeleton found with her body, only a quantity of bones. The coroner had the body; the police had the bones. I was filled in on all this, and more, by Detective Radovich, who called me with the idea that I would somehow be able to explain what had happened, since after all, Maria and I were in trouble because of Kate.

I had an idea I might know something about the bones, but I didn't share this with Radovich. It was interesting that when Kate's husband had realized she was missing, he had thought to go up the hill to the subdivision site to look for her, Why there? Also, why bones?

One way to look at it, you could say we were lucky. The Government had lost its complaining witness. With no threat of prosecution, I was free to deal with Detective Radovich's investigation. On the other hand The Z's would never be happy until they had Doctor Rayburn's head on a pole, and probably mine too, after the episode at Catalina. And I still had Cannizzarro's tape of Mozart's 'Jupiter' symphony. He would be wanting it back.

No matter what, the bones were probably the key to Kate Balducci's death. I thought back to the redwood deck, her nice tan, the powdered sugar and the imaginary reindeer. Okay, when life deals you cards, as I am fond of saying, you should play them. So I did.

The first cards to play were the papers I wound up with from my raid on the Balducci household, courtesy of Rigoberto Salas. There were two pieces of paper, a telephone long distance billing statement, and a receipt from a company called Museum Pieces, in downtown LA. One of the toll calls charged to the Balducci telephone matched the number of Museum Pieces, so I called the number from my office, using the speakerphone, with my hand-held tape recorder running, and I got the following on tape:

Me: "Hello, is this Museum Pieces?"

Somebody: "Who is this?"

Me: "My name is Harry Gillette. I wanted to order from you but I don't have your catalog.

Somebody: "Waddaya talkin' about?"

Me: (beginning to sound doubtful, things not going as planned) "Don't you have a catalog you could send me?"

Somebody: "You want to buy somethin' you don't know what it is? You're kidding me. Who is this, Howie?"

I couldn't decide whether to be Howie or not, so I hung up. Was Howie Howard Running Bear? What really got me was the voice. Lawyers do a great deal of taking on the phone, and you either get good at evaluating people by their voices and speech patterns, or you wind up as an Avon Lady. The Museum Pieces voice had been a wise guy, or someone who wanted to sound like one. Chicago, if I was any judge. Interesting, even provocative, but not immediately helpful.

Okay, next card. A bone picked at random from my

161

ample supply; a patella, I think. Again, the tiny but painfully neat little lettering in black ink. This patella was number E-12140MOW. Who writes on bones? Museums. That was what Franco Mandelbrot had told me up at Sylvan Glade. The bones came from a museum. And right in the back of the Thomas Guide, the indispensable L.A. roadmap and guidebook, there it was in a list of points of interest, the Museum of the West. MOW - it was entirely plausible. And, damn, I had even been there one Sunday with Maria, looking at a collection of Indian baskets and blankets. I didn't remember seeing any bones.

The Museum of the West was just north of downtown, in the direction of Pasadena. This was the direction in which LA's first homeward-bound commuters drove their cars; to Pasadena, up the Arroyo Seco, on the world's first freeway. The Pasadena Freeway was now hopelessly obsolete, a narrow four-lane carnival ride, with midget off ramps set at terror-inducing right angles to the traffic flow.

I drove halfway up the Arroyo Seco on the freeway and took one of the droll little off ramps. It was September, and the late morning air was still and hot. And dusty. You could sense a layer of dust on everything. Narrow tributary roads led up smaller canyons on either side of the Arroyo Seco; steep little winding roads between old wooden houses jammed in together, just like up in the Hollywood hills, but older; unstylish, ramshackle frame buildings with peeling paint, shimmering in the hot, still air. All the vegetation that wasn't cactus looked dead. Numerous old parked cars also looked dead. And in the middle of this was the Museum of the West, in a converted 1920's mansion. And in the middle of the Museum a courtyard, hot and dusty, in which I stood talking with Morris Bissette, curator of Native American artifacts. All the bones, he was telling me, were gone.

"It's Federal law. The Native American Graves Protection and Repatriation Act. We had to give away our entire collection. Each Tribe got the bones that belonged to them."

Back East, if I said curator you would imagine a little

stoop-shouldered guy with horn-rims and a tweed jacket with leather elbow patches. Morris Bissette was an overweight balding blond man in his thirties with an engaging smile but so-so teeth, a fringed buckskin vest, bluejeans, and western style ostrich-skin boots. He wore a serious array of silver and turquoise jewelry. He looked sweaty, but then I probably did too.

"It was sad, in a way, to see our entire collection go," he said. "We had material from digs going back to the twenties, from sites all over the Southwest. But we had to comply. All the museums did, at least in the US. There's a lot of material left abroad, mostly in Japan; you know the Japanese are crazy about American Indians. Or I should say Native Americans." He looked embarrassed. Was I likely to be offended by the 'I' word?

"So you had to figure out who the descendants were," I said. "Which Indians," he winced, "Native Americans were the right ones?"

"Right. The tribes were supposed to apply, but really everyone was supposed to cooperate to get the job done. Everything was supposed to be reburied." That was three 'supposed's' in two sentences.

"Yeah, but was everything reburied?"

"Well, we sure don't have any human remains left at this Museum. We couldn't. It wouldn't be legal anymore. We had a deadline." His expression changed. "Why are you asking me? Have you found something?"

Was there any point in telling this earnest curator that his precious bones were scattered all over Malibu, unburied? And probably at a crime scene at that?

"Mr. Bissette," I lied, "I'm a lawyer representing real estate developers on the West Side. One of our grading crews found some material with numbers written in ink, with the letters MOW. We were wondering if it could have come from here."

Morris Bissette took me completely by surprise; he laughed. "Hey pardner, once we give the stuff away it's not our business what happens to it." He was waving his hands at me in a 'go away' gesture. "Your clients know what to do; you've got to report it to the State, contact the Tribal representatives, whatever. Maybe we had your stuff once, but we sure ain't taking it back." He laughed again. "It could go on forever, you know? We give it to the Tribes, they bury it, your client digs it up and brings it back here. Gimme a break."

27

Museum Pieces turned out to be a tired-looking combination showroom-warehouse on Alameda, south of downtown. A blank façade on an empty street, with a heavy steel door, a buzzer and a sign instructing me to 'ring to enter.' Above the door, a little closed-circuit TV camera. After a few rings the door buzzed back at me, and I entered a dusty showroom with glass shelves on the walls holding a large assortment of dubious western artifacts. The kind of crap that shops in Beverly Hills sell to Japanese tourists. Reproduction leather holster belts and chaps with silver conchos, mounted antelope horns, fake tomahawks, flint-tipped arrows, branding irons. What were people going to do with those? And tons of beadwork, turquoise, silver, everything for the collector of Americana, and all fake as George W. Bush's reading glasses.

In two corners of the room, shirtsleeved young Hispanic men talked on cellphones, looking at me as if I might explode. I was making an effort to put out of my mind the joke about the nun, the Indian chief and the deer. Who was I going to tell it to?

The man to my left lowered his cellphone long enough to say "What joo wan?" then resumed his conversation without waiting for a reply. He talked, looked back up at me, then talked some more. I had the idea I was the subject of his conversation.

I said "I'm an Indian." They both stared at me. "From Cincinnati." I hadn't rehearsed anything. I had no idea where this was coming from, or going. Goddamn improv workshops.

Lefthand cellphone man said "Joo an Indian?" then resumed his conversation for a moment. Then he said "Wa kine?"

What kind of Indians lived in Cincinnati? I said "Alpaca." Then I said "I've been up in Malibu talking to my brothers."

This seemed to work. He closed his cellphone and nodded to righthand cellphone man, who drifted through a doorway into the warehouse area. Then he said "Joo buyin' or sellin'?"

"Selling. We've got tons of stuff. Cincinnati is digging up a whole village to build a sports stadium."

He nodded.

"Nobody knew it was there. The City had to give us everything they found, 'cause we're the Alpaca, y'see, those were our people." Trying not to think about the Fugawee Indians, keeping on message. "We've got bones, lots of them," I went on, "skeletons, old people, babies." Right about here I realized I sounded like an idiot. Then his cellphone went off.

After a minute on the phone his expression went from bored to trying to look bored and I figured my honeymoon as an Indian might be over.

He started walking toward the door to the warehouse area, gesturing with his shoulder; I was to follow. Instead, I suddenly decided to leave. I turned and attempted to negotiate the front door, which proved to require something more elaborate than a push to open. Too late. Something hit

167

the back of my head, hard, and *then* the damn door opened and I took a boot in the rear and went sailing out onto Alameda Street, just like the bum in the cartoon getting eighty-sixed from a bar.

You actually do see stars after a blow to the head. I'd read about that.

28

The insurance carrier for Leeward Marina had just agreed to buy Rigoberto Salas' head injury for one hundred thousand dollars, due, I thought, to the fact that the company was in Georgia and didn't know any better. A California insurance company wouldn't have given me that kind of money if *Señor* Salas had fallen into a vat at McDonalds and emerged as Big Macs. I quickly confirmed the settlement by email, in case the adjuster in Georgia should lose his job when the claims manager found out what he agreed to pay us. I then called Maria at work and told her of this miracle.

"Buy a bottle of Sancerre," was her response. "I have fresh Santa Barbara mussels from the Farmer's Market for tonight."

I said I would buy two bottles, and four ounces of Beluga. I have been told my caviar trick sounds precious, but I don't care; my reaction whenever I hit a horse is always immediately to buy caviar. I strongly believe in the symbolic value of food, probably due to the absence of organized religion in my life. So I celebrate life at the dinner table, and over the years Maria has come around to share my point of view. We observe these rituals at home and at local restaurants, and we visit Paris together, when we can, like devout Catholics go to Lourdes. You've got to take your spirituality where you find it.

Amazingly, the best *moules* Paris can offer are not as good as mussels from Santa Barbara, which are consistently as firm and sweet as such mollusks can get. The ones we buy at the Wednesday market are harvested and sold by a company that has a contract to clean marine growth off the legs of oil drilling platforms in the Santa Barbara Channel. This is a funny way to get fine seafood. Remember this the next time an environmentalist tells you that big oil companies are ruining the planet. It's probably true, but nothing is a total loss.

The mussels are steamed in broth, which is prepared by sautéing chopped onion and minced garlic in olive oil, then adding a cup of white wine, tomato paste, red pepper flakes Italian herbs and chopped parsley. Two pounds of cleaned mussels will take ten to fifteen minutes in a covered skillet. If they don't open, don't eat them.

By dusk we had reduced dinner to a scant half bottle of Sancerre and a large pile of mussel shells; what archaeologists call a midden. One of the things I like best about eating any shellfish is the resulting messy pile of empty shells. This is an experience we have in common with our most remote ancestors. Of course the Sancerre came much later.

Bobby Baxter's dog Captain had adopted us and was present for dinner. Bobby was usually too plastered by dinnertime to be much fun for a dog, and Maria shared everything we ate with Captain, which was definitely fun for a dog. At the moment she was attempting to introduce Captain to caviar.

I said "Imagine Russians catching huge sturgeon in

171

the Caspian Sea so that a little dog in Marina del Rey could turn up his nose at Beluga."

Maria looked at me sternly. "You're obsessing," she said. "You think because it's expensive you've got to eat it all." That was exactly what I had been thinking.

Not really," I said. "I just don't know why you insist on offering everything we eat to the dog."

She picked Captain up and held him at the table on her lap. Captain sniffed at a mussel shell. A few grains of caviar fell off his muzzle to the carpet. Maria had let her hair down from the severe French braid she wore to work, and she glowed darkly in tan cashmere and pearls.

"You know," I said, "twelve-volt lights are good for Hispanics. They're redder than one-ten."

Maria said "You think that's funny, Tom, but it's racist. Why should I spend time with you if you have no respect for my people?"

"French wine and caviar?"

"Yes, probably." It was full dark now, and quiet. "You're worried about Murray," she said, "I can tell."

"How do you do that?"

"Read you like a book?"

"Yeah."

"Well, I've known you for, what, six or seven years?

"You don't remember?"

She reached across the table and stroked my hand. "Of course I remember. You're funny."

"I do my best."

"No," she said, "I don't mean that way. It's funny how you make this big show of being Mister Logical and Mister Cynical, and that's not what you are."

"I like the 'Mister' part. You make me sound like a character in a children's book: 'The Mopey Little Puppy Meets Mister Cynical."

"Oh, that's right, I forgot Mister Smartass."

I said "I don't think they could put Mister Smartass in a children's book."

"Maybe not. But all these Misters, they're not you.

172

"They're not?"

"No, *eres buena gente* and you don't want to admit it. What's the expression; you wear your heart on your sleeve?"

"That's not something a lawyer wants to hear."

"You were a human being before you were a lawyer."

"I don't think so. Most of us weren't. I'm not sure I can remember that far back."

"*Tomas*, you're worried about your friend. Do something about it."

Nobody had seen Doctor Rayburn since we got back from Catalina, which I didn't consider to be any great loss, but nobody had seen Murray either. I had been busy working on Rigoberto Salas' case, and when I'm that absorbed I tend to go into a reactive mode; unless something intrudes into my concentration, it doesn't exist. So I really hadn't noticed that Murray didn't seem to be around. Larry Hayden had apparently lost interest in the things we had discussed on my boat that night, and Gizzi and Cannizzarro seemed to have taken a few weeks off. Why would I get so lucky?

So I picked up the phone and called Murray's boat.

"This is Murray Markoff," said the answering machine. "I'm at summer camp and I won't be home for a while. Leave a message."

I hung up. Maria and Captain were both looking a question at me. I swear the dog was too smart for the job.

"Murray's up in Pearblossom," I said.

Summer Camp was a piece of property with a trailer on it, up by Devil's Punchbowl in the High Desert just outside of L.A. Years ago somebody had donated it to the Sea Pioneers. Hersh and Murray both used it as a weekend cabin. As far as I knew, no Sea Pioneer had ever set foot there. There was no phone, a small air-cooled generator for power, and the bathroom was behind a bush. Murray called it Summer Camp, and Maria and I had used it a half dozen times in Spring, to look at the wild flowers, and sometimes to be naughty out of doors. It's only about an hour and a half out of town by car, but it's very isolated.

Maria said "If Murray's up in the Desert he's got

173

Doctor Rayburn with him."

It was a reasonable surmise. There would be no better place to hide. There's no phone number for someone to try to trace; nobody got mail there. Pearblossom consists of a gas station, a convenience store and a realty office, at a crossroads in the void, and the Pioneers' property isn't even in the town itself.

Maria said "Does Murray still have a cell phone?"

"Wouldn't matter. There's no reception at the trailer, remember?

"How about the neighbor," she said. "The maniac. What's his name? Carruthers?

Carruthers was an amiable survivalist who had a house up a dirt road from the Pioneers' property, and used an easement across it to get to the County road. Though deranged, he had always been a good neighbor, happy to help. He lived on a disability pension from the military, and spent his time at home, converting semiautomatic weapons to full automatic and selling them discreetly at swap meets. Never know when you're going to need a real machine gun. I called him and he confirmed recent activity at Summer Camp. Lights on at night when he went up the road to his house, etcetera. I asked him to stop by the next time he went down the hill, and an hour later, Murray called me back from Carruthers' place.

"Where've you been, Tom? I'm shittin' a brick up here. I'm with this bum Doctor day and night for a week now. He's scared, I'm scared. We've got twenty-seven dollars left between us. Hersh says my dock is crawling with all kindsa people don't belong there. He says he's afraid to go to work. I can't go home, I got checks in the mail, and my friend here, he doesn't even have a home. You wanna take a little responsibility, Tommy? Help us straighten this out? I'm an old Jew. Living in a trailer gives me *schpilkes*."

"Murray," I said, "wait a minute. Is the Doctor there?"

"Oh, the Docteh? My son the docteh?" For a moment Murray was a mocking Borscht Belt comic, then he dropped it. "The son of a bitch, he's right here. Hold the phone."

174

"Mr. McGuire?"

"Tom. Listen, the files you were telling me about when you were on my boat? Where are they?"

"You mean the records of the cosmetic surgeries I did for Mr. Cannizzarro's friends?

"Yeah, those. What happened to them?"

"I'm not sure. I think my wife has them."

I said "You mean your ex-wife?"

"Of course. It's funny how I keep saying that. She's the only wife I ever had."

"But she divorced you," I said. "How did she wind up with files from your office?"

I could hear him sigh. "I went up to my office at night a few days before I was supposed to be killed in the carjacking, and all the files were gone. My wife's lawyer had subpoenaed them for a court hearing. They wanted me held in contempt for not paying her spousal support, and she wanted the Judge to raise the amount I was supposed to pay her every month. So her lawyer said he was going to use my files to prove how much money I was making. I think he was just trying to put pressure on me. The guy was a professional sadist. All through the divorce he never stopped thinking up ways to drive me crazy. My lawyer was never aggressive enough to keep up with him. All he could do was charge me more money. If it wasn't for the divorce, I might not have listened to Mr. Hayden. Right now I'd settle for my wife's divorce lawyer."

"But the files with the photographs," I said, "that was what Larry, Mr. Hayden, wanted, wasn't it? And you to give testimony about them?"

"Of course."

"And they let it get away from them like that?"

"The Witness Protection Program isn't as organized as they want you to think." He said this without a hint of sarcasm. "We assumed the files were in my office. They weren't, and by the time I found that out, the carjacking was all set up for two days later and there was no time to look for files. For a while we thought Mr. Gizzi had taken them." He

175

paused. "Did you see what they did to my lovely car?"

His lovely car? He must have seen the TV coverage of his own carjacking.

I said "So what happened after that?"

"Don't you see," he was angry now, "after that I was dead, God damn it. What could I do? And I forgot to change my will. Right after the carjacking I remembered she would get everything. I was so mad. I wanted to write a new will leaving everything to my brother, but Mr. Hayden wouldn't let me do it. He said it was too risky, and I wouldn't be able to get the signatures back-dated to before I died. I heard she got almost nothing for the car. She stopped paying rent on my office, sold all my equipment, state of the art examination tables, the works. Didn't even try to sell the practice. She could have gotten real money for it."

"Didn't they try to find the files after the carjacking?"

"They talked about it, but after a few days I was in Dallas working as a paramedic, and you know what happened there." He paused, and I could hear Murray and Carruthers talking in the background. "If my wife's lawyer found out I was still alive do you have any idea how much money I would owe in spousal support by now?"

"Don't worry," I said. "If your ex-wife's lawyer found out you were still alive, he'd keep it a deep dark secret."

"Why would he do that? He hates me."

"She'd have to give back the life insurance."

"Oh Jesus."

29

"The main reason we came to see you is because of the accusations against you and your friend. Kate told me she couldn't see much from the house, only enough to describe the boat, and to hear gunfire. To her, if you were out there shooting guns you were an enemy of the environment, a redneck trying to kill something. She hated guns. And she could see you were fishing, that was no good either. She told me she didn't realize how much trouble you were going to get into."

"So she sent her friend to vandalize my boat?"

He was embarrassed. "Please understand, Mr. McGuire, we've just come from my wife's funeral. It's hard for me to be objective. Katie didn't think of it as vandalism. She thought it was an opportunity to help the whales, more than just going to demonstrations, handing out leaflets, you know. Look,..." He was on the verge of tears "...I loved her. I know what she did was stupid."

Victor Balducci and his father-in-law Franco Mandelbrot sat solemnly, side by side in my client chairs, in plain dark suits and ties, having just returned from Kate Balducci's funeral service. Her ashes had been scattered at sea. I thought of the corpse with the navy tattoo, the stand-in for Doctor Rayburn, who had also been cremated and scattered at sea. Doctor Rayburn's stunt double, I suppose you could say. Balducci was telling me the graffiti artist on whom I had dropped an anchor had been Kate's sidekick, and that his death had caused her a complete change of heart.

"She met him at a rally in Malibu," Balducci said, "against the County sewer project. You remember that?" I did. Malibu residents were against anything that would lead to further development of Malibu. All those multi-million-dollar homes were attached to septic systems; no sewers at all. This led to a certain fragrance in the air around the Malibu Colony when the weather was warm, but it also radically reduced the possible development. Big hotels meant big waste disposal needs. No sewers meant no hotels, no apartment buildings.

Balducci said "She read a book a few years ago that influenced her thinking, *The Monkey Wrench Gang*, about ecoterrorism. Do you know it?"

I told him I did. It was a lively presentation of the moral imperative for fucking up heavy equipment, so that machinery self-destructed when evil people tried using it to destroy portions of the planet. I have always been wary of an attitude of moral superiority, though, no matter how tempting the cause. As it has been written: 'great oafs from tiny icons grow.'

Balducci said "She started on a great crusade. Half the stuff she wanted to do I had to talk her out of. I'm in the D.A.'s office, for Chrissakes, but I'm at work all day, and plenty of weekends. You can't treat your wife like a child." Even though she is one, his expression said.

Mandelbrot said "She never needed to do anything for herself. I guess it's fairly typical. I came up the hard way, so

179

she never had to strain herself."

I thought of his wedding present of the beach house. Give me one of those and I wouldn't get much done either.

"In any case," he went on, "you killed her buddy."

There was no sense of accusation; no rancor. Neither man looked upset by my deed. I had done them a favor by slowing Kate down.

Balducci said "She read about the body being recovered, and she was distraught. The guy was a folksinger. Phil something. I think the business with your boat was her idea. He could never have figured out how to get in so much trouble without her. I came home from work and she was in shock. She told me everything. There was a lot more than I had suspected. Some vandalism, painting slogans on buildings, like on your boat, but the shocker was the bones. I hadn't heard about that before." Mandelbrot stirred in his chair. This was the most painful part for him. I remembered his attempt to quote Shakespeare to me at Sylvan Glade: 'how sharper than a serpent's tooth it is...'

Mandelbrot said "You know what the Native American thing has become in Malibu?"

I said I wasn't sure.

"Malibu has a City Archaeologist and a Cultural Heritage Officer. How many cities in California do you think have goofballs like that on the payroll? It's really the same as the sewer business; if there's Native American artifacts and remains all over Malibu, well, then you can't build anything there, can you? I don't know how long she'd been at it, but Kate had figured it out, and somehow she was getting Native American stuff, artifacts, bones, human bones. She and her friends were burying the stuff anywhere they thought there was going to be development."

I said "Where were they getting the bones?"

Mandelbrot and his son-in-law looked at each other.

Balducci said "That's one of the reasons why we're here."

"You think I gave her bones?"

I tried for outraged innocence; did ok, considering.

Nobody said anything for a moment. I buzzed Cathy for coffee. Mandelbrot asked permission and lit a cigar. I tried a different question.

"What did Detective Radovich tell you about me?"

Another look passed between them. I could sense the echo of some discussion about my possible role in Kate Balducci's murder.

Mandelbrot was one of those smokers who leads the conversation with his cigar. He signaled his entrance and spoke.

"What we say here is in confidence. We didn't think it would be wise to tell the Detective too much. For instance, the man who drowned. Kate could have been criticized for that, no? After all, she put him up to it." I thought of Charles Manson. "Also," he went on, "about the bones. We were told that my daughter's body was found near some bones. And you, Mr. McGuire..." he paused for some delicate cigar business, "...you brought a bone up to Sylvan Glade, to our meeting." He smiled at the memory. "I almost hit you with it, I'm sorry to say."

"I remember that." Any sarcasm I might have intended was lost in a swirl of cigar smoke.

"You told me the bone came from Katie's truck. I could ask you how you happened to have it," he continued, "if I wanted to pry into your affairs. Or I could assume that all of these bones might have come from the same place, and ask you if you know who killed my daughter."

I couldn't tell whether I was being accused of murder or being asked for help. Mandelbrot was a veteran negotiator of major real estate deals, and his face revealed nothing. His son-in-law had become preoccupied with my truly breathtaking view of the Marina. I looked at Franco's cigar for guidance but it was motionless in his hand.

I had already decided not to turn my back on the disaster that had befallen the Environmental Lady, but what happened next was still a surprise to me. I told my two visitors about Howard Running Bear and the Malibu Band of the Chumash Nation. I told them about Morris Bissette and

181

the Museum of the West, and about the cellphone goons at Museum Pieces. I held back only *Señor* Salas' theft of bones from the Mandelbrot Development truck. But why tell them the rest? I felt sorry for them. I felt sorry for myself, for Maria. I didn't appreciate getting hit on the head, kicked in the ass and thrown out into Alameda Street, getting my boat vandalized. Take your pick.

I had just made some money on Rigoberto Salas' case and could leave the office alone for awhile without economic self-destruction. The whole thing fascinated me. That was probably at the root of it all; that and a lingering zest for catching bad guys, left over from my days at the US Attorney's Office. Of course, when I worked there my official position on the war between law enforcement and crooks was that it didn't matter who won; it was a game. It's funny that the existential viewpoint to which I have adhered so proudly can dissolve in an instant before the seduction of occupying the moral high ground. Also, I remembered the day I drove up Pacific Coast Highway to meet Franco Mandelbrot at Sylvan Glade, with a femur in my attaché case. Dammit, that was a funny day.

Some hands are too entertaining to fold. I know this makes for a lousy poker player. I'll cop to it. What you really want to watch out for in this world isn't evil, it's boredom. Some people can go to the office and turn the crank every day and not get tired of it. I am not one of those people. Sue me.

When I had concluded my story, Balducci informed us that Howard Running Bear had been a frequent visitor in their home.

"He's an Indian like I'm the Pope,' he said, "but I couldn't say anything. Kate would have blown up at me. She thought I looked down on her friends. She said being a prosecutor made me cynical. Actually, I thought a lot of her friends were bums; too busy saving the Planet to get a job."

Mandelbrot said "So the bones they were burying, they got them from him?"

I hadn't actually said that. He thought for a moment.

"You know, I had to hire someone from that Malibu Chumash Company to monitor the grading we did in Malibu." A pause. He made a wry face. "Aw shit, I was paying them to look out for things we might uncover with our bulldozers and what, they were giving the stuff to Katie to put there in the first place?"

We sat together for a minute or two. Mandelbrot smoked his cigar. He looked overcome at the magnitude of his daughter's secret life.

I said "But nobody ever found any Indian remains on the Malibu subdivision."

"Yeah they did," Balducci said, "with her body." He paused for a moment. "So if Katie had been getting Indian bones from this Running Bear guy, what if she went up the hill to meet with him after her friend drowned, and told him she was through. She could have screwed up his whole operation, and I think she would have, considering how sorry she felt."

I said "So he killed her?"

So there it was. On an impulse I looked up the Malibu Band of the Chumash Nation in the white pages. To my surprise they lived in a high-rise office building in Century City.

30

Century City is not a retirement community, as the name might suggest, but a pod of high-rise office towers built on the site of the original 20th Century Fox film lot in West Los Angeles. Century City is as close as Los Angeles gets to Brasilia; the city of tomorrow. Everything that isn't a high-rise is a sidewalk, making an environment that lacks all human scale. A walk through Century City makes you feel like an ant on the pavement, and the densely populated high-rise office towers suggest ant farms, the tall slender plastic boxes of sand in which I tried to establish ant colonies as a child. My ants always died. The ants of Century City flourish and grow fat in Armani suits.

The Malibu Band of the Chumash Nation occupied quarters at 2049 Avenue of the Stars; one of Century City's tallest buildings. I drove down a ramp into the parking garage, which seemed to be as large as Zimbabwe and which strongly reinforced the ant farm motif. What could be more antlike than to crawl through these ever-extending tunnels, deeper and deeper into the maze? I parked at a remote location far below street level, a place called Red South Twelve. The bright breezy late summer morning was left far behind. No weather down here, bub, just us ants.

On the 44th floor, The shiny metallic letters on a pair of bulky mahogany doors might just as well have spelled ACME REALTY AND INVESTMENTS, but these said CHUMASH NATION. Whatever went on in there, it was businesslike. The receptionist was Anglo, and spoke with an English accent; the epitome of L.A. chic. The reception area was furnished with standard upscale waiting room stuff; chrome, glass, leather upholstered furniture. There were rugs instead of the standard broadloom, but they were the kind of Indian rugs that come from India.

The walls were covered with hand-woven blankets and tapestries, and there were glass display cases holding the same kinds of dubious artifacts I had seen at Museum Pieces, dramatically illuminated. The remaining space on the walls was filled with framed photographs and documents.

It was certainly true that the place looked very anthropological. The thing was, it didn't feel permanent. In L.A. lots of things feel impermanent, but when I worked for the Government I would sometimes visit a business I was investigating, then come back a month later and find it was gone; empty rooms and, sometimes, an irate landlord screwed for the rent. If you see enough of this kind of thing you get a feeling for it, and I had that feeling as I told the receptionist what I wanted.

I was expected, and Mr. Running Bear would see me, but not right away, which gave me a chance to examine the show. There were many photographs of people wearing what I assumed were traditional Chumash costumes, dancing or participating in ceremonies. In some shots I recognized prominent members of the entertainment industry. These were Malibu residents, I realized, appreciating Malibu's cultural heritage, and defending their turf. In L.A. every dry cleaner has its wall of celebrity head shots, autographed to

185

the proprietor. Even Doctor Rayburn's office. Why should the Chumash Nation be any different?

There was a photograph of former Mayor Riordan shaking hands with a person I decided had to be Howard Running Bear, a handsome youngish man who looked kind of Italian, in a really nice silk suit, shoulder length straight black hair and feathered headband. Another picture of Charlton Heston shaking hands with the same guy.

A second set of bulky mahogany doors opened and the youngish man in the really nice silk suit appeared. It was Howard Running Bear, as I had assumed. He looked even better than his photographs. He had a dark complexion, and actually did look Italian; Roman nose, long straight black hair pulled back into a braid, but the most prominent feature was the bright, clear gaze of a health guru, or maybe an aerobics instructor. He radiated positive thinking and first class dental work, which went well with the suit. I suddenly found myself wondering what, after all, I was doing there. I had the damn femur in my inside jacket pocket. Mandelbrot had considerately given it back to me in my office. It had gotten me in trouble once and I was thinking it was going to get me in trouble again.

We sat in Howard Running Bear's inner office, which was even more intensely decorated with Native American materials of all kinds, including a free-standing life-sized Chumash tribesman. I assumed it was a statue and not taxidermy, but didn't have the nerve to ask.

He turned sideways in his swivel chair to give me the profile.

"So," he said. He appeared to be speaking directly to the Chumash tribesman standing next to the desk, poised in the middle of a dance. "You told me on the phone you had something you thought might belong to me."

This had been my ploy to get the appointment. I reached into my jacket pocket and pulled out the femur.

"Yes," I said, "if this is what I think it is."

I handed the femur across his desk and he studied it briefly, rotating it to examine the inked-on notations, then he looked up and laughed.

"Shit," said Howard Running Bear, "these things turn up everywhere."

"They do?" I was dumbfounded. The last time I did the femur fandango, at Sylvan Glade, it had enraged a naked real estate developer. I obviously wasn't looking for more of the same, but laughter?

He said "This is from the Museum of the West, right?"

"Yes," I said. "I've already been there. That's where I learned what it was."

He laughed some more. "We've got tons of this stuff," he said. "You didn't find this in the ground. I know that. We clean the ink off before we rebury them. By the way, you don't want this back, right? We can keep it? Because one way or the other you're not supposed to have it."

I assured him I didn't want to keep the bone. After all, he wasn't the only one who had tons of the stuff. It seemed curious, though, that he didn't want to know where I had gotten it.

Now," he continued, smiling, "if you had found this in the ground at a construction site we'd have to do some work for you, or for somebody. Most anywhere around here, if you turned up a bone like this, the law is you would have to stop right there; hang up your shovel, turn off the bulldozer, whatever. Then we could do an archaeological review."

"I thought you were an Indian tribe."

"That's not a simple question, Mr. McGuire. The only Chumash tribe recognized by the Federal Government is in San Ynez on a reservation. We have an application pending, you know, like when it says 'patent pending?'"

Evidently a well-worn little joke.

I said "Pending with who?"

"It's not a who," Howard Running Bear said, "it's a what. The Branch of Acknowledgment and Research, Bureau of Indian Affairs, Department of the Interior. There are over one hundred and sixty applications pending from unrecognized tribes. It can take years, and it can cost a fortune."

"But when you're all finished you get a gambling casino, right?"

This struck a sour note with Howard Running Bear. My response was inappropriate. He frowned.

"This is not about gambling casinos, sir." Suddenly he sounded like Jesse Jackson. "We are a people who have been decimated by the White Man, and our culture all but obliterated from the earth. Then the tragic remains of a great nation is dug up and despoiled by the same people who practiced genocide on us in the first place. How would you like to see your great-great grandmother's bones on view in a museum, in a glass case, with the treasured possessions she took to her grave?"

He had a point, but it raised another interesting question.

"So whenever the bones or artifacts turn up in construction sites, or in museums, you get them back?"

"Right," he said, "Under the Native American Graves Protection and Repatriation Act, if it's in a museum that receives Federal money. California has laws of its own, but either way, we get the bones back. You don't have to be an officially recognized tribe to accept ancient artifacts and remains."

"Then if you re-bury all that stuff, where would the bone I brought you have come from?. The man at the museum told me he gave it to you."

Morris Bissette had said no such thing, but he wouldn't know the difference.

Dark clouds again obscured Howard Running Bear's sunny disposition. Our meeting was coming to a close.

"Look, mister whoever you are, don't come back here asking any more questions, okay? But just so you'll understand, the law makes them give the stuff back to us. It doesn't say what we have to do with it. The White Man desecrated the graves of our ancestors. It's not the White Man's business what happens later. I could take this-" he held up the femur I had brought him "-and make souvenir keychains out of it if I wanted to."

188

"Or sell it," I said, "to a company called Museum Pieces?"

Got him.

"Or maybe sell it to Kate Balducci?"

Got him again. "Did you know she died?"

"What?"

"Someone killed her."

"Who? What are you talking about?"

"Kate Balducci. They found her body up on her father's subdivision in Malibu, with a bunch of old bones, your kind of bones. You know," I said in a friendly, confiding sort of way, "there are people who actually think you killed her."

Howard Running Bear pushed at some buttons on his phone, probably attempting to summon aid, then thought better of it, stood at his gigantic desk and pointed over my shoulder. "Out," he said. "Now." He seemed upset. No noticeable reaction from the dancing Chumash tribesman.

I was halfway through the reception area when he called out to me from his office doorway.

"It would be a good idea if you stayed away from the Chumash people in the future."

I stopped and turned back. "Why is that?"

"Because if you don't you're going to have Indian trouble."

A few minutes later I sat in my car at Red South Twelve musing on Howard Running Bear's last comment. 'Indian trouble' sounded like a movie with John Wayne in it. An old Catskill Mountains piece of business kept crowding into my mind, the kind you can't do any more:

TOURIST ON AN INDIAN RESERVATION MEETS THE
CHIEF, RAISES HER HAND IN THE AIR AND SAYS 'HOW.'
HE RAISES HIS HAND AND SAYS 'SOME.'
SHE SAYS 'I THOUGHT YOU INDIANS SAID 'HOW.'
HE SAYS 'ME KNOW HOW... ME WANT SOME.'

And so did Howard Running Bear. When that joke was

189

written Indians were supposed to talk funny. That's gone, along with the black characters who say things like 'Ah laks liver worstest, and ass bestus.' White comedians can't do this kind of material any more. Someday, when you've got time on your hands, try writing comedy that doesn't slam some person or group. It's not impossible but it's not easy either.

Having involuntarily googled my brain for Indian jokes there was no way to stop this one:

FIRST BANANA: I WAS SITTING IN A HOTEL LOBBY AND AN INDIAN CAME IN.
SECOND BANANA: AN INDIAN? DID HE HAVE A RESERVATION?"

Sorry. Sometimes I can't help myself.

I started up the car and eased my way through the dimly lit tunnels upward toward the light. Before I got too far I found myself boxed in behind a black Lincoln Town Car. Just like Gizzi's and Cannizzarro's, I thought, but black. As I watched, the trunk of the Lincoln popped open, then two weightlifter types got out of the car, one on each side. They looked like a matched pair; mid twenties, long black hair, with the kind of heavy arms and shoulders that evoke the word 'engorged.' They didn't look at me, but took baseball bats out of the open trunk and started smashing the front end of my car. Nothing vicious; a work assignment. I locked myself in. The driver of the car behind me sounded a complaining horn. Maybe he couldn't see what was happening to me. You'd think he could have given me a hand.

I've never been too attached to my car, an aging Jaguar sedan bartered to me by a client, a nice old man who owed me money and couldn't pay. So my immediate thought was to jump out of the vehicle and run for it. But would they turn their bats on me?

Some years back it had become fashionable among certain groups in the Los Angeles area to shoot at cars on the freeway. In response to this threat I got the idea that I

190

needed to keep a loaded pistol in my front seat. 'For protection,' I had explained to Maria, who fortunately talked me out of this lunatic proposition. Anyway, it was seriously illegal, and me a lawyer, et cetera. But if I became the target of violence while in my car I insisted that I would need to defend myself, and I had purchased a marine flare pistol for this purpose. It's made out of red plastic and looks like a toy gun and fires an aerial flare that looks a little like a shotgun shell. It's very low velocity compared to a firearm, and won't penetrate anything, but the flare burns hot, and it burns long. It's not a weapon, it's emergency safety equipment for boats. The Coast Guard requires them.

So I stepped out of my car, flare gun in hand, and put a round neatly into the Lincoln's open trunk, where something caught fire. The two immediately stopped beating on my car, although there wasn't much left to bash by then, and ran back toward the Lincoln. As I took off on foot down the ramp in the other direction I heard one of them shout something about a fire extinguisher. Evidently, the fire extinguisher was in the trunk, with the fire. When I turned around for one last look, the Lincoln was well engulfed in flames and the two men seemed to be dancing around it.

It wasn't the car, and I'm not sure if it was Kate Balducci, but that afternoon was when I decided what would become of Howard Running Bear, if not exactly how it would happen.

31

We were having breakfast in the aft cockpit, looking at the Catalina pictures. The camera Cannizzarro had taken from me and thrown in the water at Isthmus Cove was advertised as waterproof; not the sort of claim you'd ever want to test. But Bobby Baxter had obligingly fished it out of the water at the gas dock, and returned it to me days later in the Marina. The pictures had survived in perfect condition.

Maria held up a shot of me in my bathing suit on the beach at Cat Harbor. She took a sip of coffee.

"You still look good," she said, somehow managing to suggest the phrase 'in spite of everything.'

She looked better, in a shot I had taken of her in a heart-stopping string bikini on *Den Mother's* foredeck, sunning herself at Isthmus Cove. There was a shot of Murray in a Hawaiian shirt and jeans, looking very 'on vacation' on the patio in front of the restaurant at Isthmus Cove.

It was early and still quiet in C Basin, except for the

193

rumble of jets taking off at LAX and the occasional diver going by in an outboard-powered inflatable. We had pastries purchased the night before from a new French bakery that had opened on Washington Boulevard.

The photo I had taken of Gizzi, Cannizzarro and Larry Hayden in the cockpit of the yellow offshore racer did not look like a vacation picture. It looked like a bunch of people who were up to something. Vic was facing away from the camera, but Lou was clearly recognizable. His diamond bracelet had caught the flash and looked like a band of neon around his wrist.

I was delighted to notice that Larry Hayden was wearing a Buccaneer Days tee shirt. In addition to the date and the phrase 'Buccaneer Days - Isthmus Cove', it featured a large white skull and crossbones on a black field. Larry the pirate.

The more I looked at the photograph the more I realized its potential. Did the U.S. Attorney's office know Larry had been on a boat ride with the Mob? Even if they knew, would they like the idea that I had a picture of it? Same concept with Gizzi and Cannizzarro. How much tolerance would their bosses have for the idea that these not terribly bright soldiers of misrule were going on field trips with an Assistant U.S. Attorney? No matter what anyone knew, or thought they knew about this particular boat ride, it seemed possible that circulation of this picture would jeopardize the employment situations of all of the people caught by my camera on the deck of the Cigarette. You could see an awareness of this problem in their faces. The image frozen on my film had acquired its own energy, in the strange way that photographs do. It wasn't just a picture, it was something entirely new; a reality that had not existed before.

Maria said "Don't you need to show a picture of Doctor Rayburn to that Detective? So he'll see he isn't dead?"

I said "You mean Radovich? Larry already told him the carjacking was a sham, but he'd like to see Rayburn with his own eyes. Don't worry about it."

She took another sip of coffee. Mocha Java.

She said "You mean 'don't worry your pretty little

194

head, honey? Your pretty little empty head?'"

"Oh, stop. Drink your coffee before it gets cold."

"Yes. Please forgive me, oh mighty keeper of the penis. Are we having a three dwarf morning?"

"What's that?"

"Grumpy, Sleepy and Dopey."

"Humpf."

Maria said "The reason I brought it up is that Detective Radovich is standing up there on the seawall right now, looking at our boat. See him?"

I looked up. She was right; there he was.

Rather than entertaining Detective Radovich on board, I poured an extra cup of coffee and took it up to the seawall where he was standing. Today he looked like a retired sports coach, in a baseball cap, chinos and high tops, and a tee shirt bearing the legend 'L.A. County Employees 10K Run for Muscular Dystrophy.' His eyes reflected a policeman's patience and indifference.

I said "You did a ten-k run?"

He snorted. "You're joking. The last time I ran I was in a burning building. Thanks for the coffee."

"Sorry no doughnuts."

"I'll live. Look, McGuire, I was up in Malibu the other day on top of a mountain, wondering how you got so lucky, so I thought I'd come down and ask you."

"Lucky? You mean Kate Balducci?"

"Yeah. You kind of won the lottery there, dincha?"

I said "Well, Detective, the way I look at it, if the Government thought someone had hit a witness to keep her from testifying, I'd be feeding coffee to the FBI right now, not to you. The fact that you're here tells me they don't like me for it. So you don't like me for it."

"Of course I don't. You think I'm an idiot?" He sipped his coffee. "But there is something connecting you to the victim, and something else, I forgot. I heard something about your car. There was a vehicle fire in an underground garage in Century City yesterday, and your car was there, all banged up. And somebody with a weird name, Chief piss-in-your-ear, complained you had created a disturbance in his office. Wouldn't file a complaint. What was that all about?"

195

"You gonna read me my Miranda rights?"

"Oh, shit, forget it." He sipped his coffee and looked annoyed. "I'm down here talking to you because I've got nowhere to go with the Balducci homicide. I've got pressure to do something. Her husband's in the D.A.'s office, for Chrissakes, and her father's a West Side real estate hotshot." He paused. "There's nothing. She had no enemies as far as we know. Her husband won't talk to us. Who would want to kill her?"

"Indians."

"Huh?"

"Indians. The Malibu Band of the Chumash Nation."

"Wait a minute, let me guess; Chief piss-in-your-ear?"

"What if?"

"Yeah, what the fuck if? You tell me."

"You want more coffee?"

"Ah, I'll just piss all morning. It's good coffee, though. Don't get me wrong."

"Mocha Java."

"You bet."

So I told Detective Radovich about Morris Bissette and the Museum of the West and suggested that the bones that had been found with Kate Balducci's body had probably come from the Museum's collection via Howard Running Bear, who I thought may have known the victim. I thought that was enough for the time being.

Radovich said "How come you know so much about old bones?"

"I'm an amateur archeologist."

"Okay, never mind. It'll give me something to do. You know, she fought with her assailant before she died. We got blood and tissue samples from under her fingernails. If I match it up I can close the file."

I said "Like you say, it'll give you something to do. By the way, you're not still chasing your ass on the Rayburn carjacking case, are you?"

"Yeah, kinda, but not for the homicide, 'cause there was no homicide. We found out the guy's alive."

"So no crime, then."

"Not exactly. You can't stage a fake crime in a public

place, and shoot up a car with double-aught buckshot. What if some citizen had tried to be a hero and gotten himself shot? And what about the police and medical emergency personnel and vehicles on the scene that could have been useful somewhere else? And it's illegal to file a false death certificate, and there's more; that's just the best part."

"Larry Hayden told you the whole story, then."

"Yeah, yeah, but you don't realize where it puts me. I'm a detective; I get paid to solve crimes. You think my boss wants to file criminal charges against the U.S. Marshal's Service? They're the ones who committed the crime. If I put that in a report it would be my ass."

"So, forget it."

"Two problems, McGuire. First of all, this case fucks up my clearance rate. It's an unsolvable crime. Second, the reason it's against the law to discharge a firearm in the street in L.A. County is because it's dangerous. Someone could get hurt. You think I want some fartass bureaucrats down in the Federal Building playing cops and robbers in my backyard with real bullets?"

We watched a pelican do a Kamikaze dive into the water and emerge with a fish in its beak.

Radovich said "You know what worries me? Once people in the Government start making up stuff, where does it stop? You got some doctor supposed to be dead but he isn't. There was somebody DOA at the V.A. hospital. They had a dead body down there; I saw it. Who was that, some poor slob who didn't pay his taxes? The unknown soldier?"

I said "What if somebody in the Marshal's Service wrote you a letter admitting they had set up the Rayburn carjacking, promising not to do it again, and asking you to keep it quiet?"

"Well, they'd never be able to fuck around in L.A. County as long as I was on the job. I could get a promotion with that kind of clout. But it'll never happen. If anyone in the Government ever wrote me a letter like that I'd eat your shorts in Macy's window."

I said "Lyndon Johnson had an expression to describe when someone was completely under his control. He'd say

197

'I've got his pecker in my pocket.'"

"I love it."

"Okay, I'll make you a deal. Help me run a little errand and I'll put you where you want to be."

"Is this where I have to eat your shorts?"

"Nothing as embarrassing as that."

32

A be Hochfleisher looked like he was made of beef jerky, except for his skin color, which was gray. Fifty years of practicing divorce law in Los Angeles had left him stringy and tough. He had made a fortune representing movie stars and entertainment industry executives and their wives and lovers, who were made to jump through hoops like dazed circus animals as Abe stood there like a ringmaster, firing blanks and cracking a whip. He was still the best in town. By now he was probably a little crazy.

Outside his office, on Hollywood Boulevard, grimy shops sold dildos to locals and Harley Davidson tee shirts to tourists. The street had been dug up for a subway and never restored, causing a permanent traffic jam. It was no longer a stylish address but Abe didn't need one. His office walls were crammed with framed newspaper clippings and trophy photographs; Abe with a variety of beautiful women and every entertainment executive and leading man who had ever allowed his dick to lead him astray in movieland. They all came to Abe, and always would. With any luck he would die in Court.

"Okay, boys," Abe Hochfleisher said, "what do you want?"

As Detective Radovich and I sat in Abe's client chairs, Radovich told the divorce lawyer about the plastic surgery records the proctologist had kept, and explained that he needed them for an investigation. He told the lawyer only the bare minimum. I had been introduced as 'McGuire.' I was supposed to be a cop too.

Abe Hochfleisher said "I can tell you that I did represent Mrs. Rayburn when she sued for divorce."

I knew that already from publicly available Court records. It was how we had found Abe.

"But the stuff you're looking for doesn't exist. And if it does exist I don't know where it is. And if I knew where it was I wouldn't give it to you. You're not the first people to come around here looking for those files." Those files? "There was a little puke from the Government. I sent him away too." He looked up toward the ceiling as though the Government man might be hanging there. "You know, she owes me a lot of money. I told her I would collect my fee from her husband. She didn't think his getting killed should change that. And she didn't need a divorce anymore, did she, so fuck me."

Detective Radovich explained about Gizzi and Cannizzarro, just enough to give Abe the idea.

"I'll tell you what," Radovich said, "send us away empty and you can deal with them."

Abe swiveled his chair around and looked out the window at the greasy outlines of the Hollywood Hills, shimmering in the afternoon haze. He was no stranger to extortion. He turned his chair back toward us and sat up straight.

"No can do, boys." He looked at his watch. "Look, I need to make a phone call. Don't leave just yet. Get some coffee and I'll show you where you can wait for me."

I was about to ask him what good it would do to wait around, until I caught Radovich's eye. He was making a 'simmer down' gesture with his hand. So I said nothing as we were led to the office coffee machine, then deposited in a nearly empty side office, and the door closed.

When we were alone I asked Detective Radovich what was going on.

"Look," he said.

One wall of the room was stacked almost to the ceiling with file storage boxes. Most of them had the word "Rayburn" written on them. I quickly confirmed they were the contents of Doctor Rayburn's office files, about twenty-five boxes of them. It took me a sweaty half-hour to find the plastic surgery records. They were all in the same storage box, and stood out because none of the proctology files had photographs in them. Thank God.

It turned out there were fourteen files; fourteen examples of Doctor Rayburn's skills as a part-time plastic surgeon. If the photographs were any guide, the results had been uneven.

I said "Diane Arbus would have loved these."

"Who's that?"

"She photographed freaks."

Some of the 'after' pictures were so bad it was amazing the patients hadn't murdered Doctor Rayburn on the spot.

Radovich said "I guess if these guys were on the lam, they were better off even if they didn't like how they turned out."

I held up a particularly awful one. "Would you rather have your face look like a plate of meatballs, or do three to five in the Pen?"

"It would be a close call. I don't like Italian food." He held up a photograph and made a face. "Some of these guys I'd lock up for being ugly. Look, if you've got all the files, let's get out of here."

"What do we do, just walk out with them?"

"Sure as shit." Radovich smiled. "I got a feeling there's nobody here but us."

We walked out of the little office, down the hall and through the reception area. A telephone was ringing, but no one was there to answer it. Radovich was right. Abe Hochfleisher's office was deserted.

33

You can't find the Mafia in the Yellow Pages, but it's not a problem in West Los Angeles; you can just reserve a table at Fratianne's, on Santa Monica Boulevard. Unless you're on probation. It's a standard condition of probation that you can't associate with known criminals or be in places where they congregate, so Fratianne's would be out. It was the kind of place street hoodlums call a 'rug joint'; a Maitre D, wine racks on the walls, cloth napkins, checkered tablecloths, lithographed views of Italy, and in the kitchen a fierce loyalty to fats and oils. I knew I could find at least one of the Z's there if I had the nerve to try.

The house specialty was mussels marinara; a phrase which could have served as a nickname for many of the regulars; bulky young men with conservative haircuts, dressed mostly in leather jackets tailored like a man's suit coat, over business shirts open at the neck. The Dapper Don look *du jour*. They resembled earnest, effective young car

204

salesmen who might break your legs if that's what it took to get you into a new Toyota. They projected a difficult-to-achieve balance of sincere and smartass.

Hersh was my dinner companion. Maria had refused to go. I had plans for Hersh and needed a chance to discuss things with him, and I had business with Gizzi and Cannizzarro.

Hersh had been camping out in the Sea Pioneers' classic Elco sedan cruiser after strangers had started turning up at the clubhouse, asking questions. He had moved the boat from the Pioneers' dock to a remote slip at the California Yacht Club, the most prestigious in Marina del Rey, and the one with the best security.

Hersh picked at a breadstick, dropping crumbs on Fratianne's red-and-white checkered tablecloth. He was wearing a dark blue banker's suit, with vest, a sincere trust-me expression and a red silk jacquard tie, a costume no doubt left over from his days as a promoter. There was Muzak in the background; traditional Italian favorites on the accordion.

"I can't go near my apartment," Hersh was telling me. "I can't go to the clubhouse. Everywhere I go there's some stooge or other. They want me to know they're watching."

"You know where Murray is?"

"He called. He's with Rayburn, but he wouldn't tell me where they were. I guess they're both up in the desert, on the property. Someone came by and got some money for him. His social security checks. I let him into Murray's boat at night to get clothes."

"Are you sure that was a good idea?"

A breadstick shattered in Hersh's hands. A waiter brought antipasto.

"I'm not sure of anything," he said. "I'm taking Xanax. I'm not there to accept donations. We've missed out on three boats in the last ten days. That I know of. I'm too old for this."

"That's what Murray says."

Over Hersh's shoulder I saw Lou Gizzi enter the

205

restaurant with two or three other men. He looked over at me, turned around and walked back out the door. To make a phone call, probably. It wouldn't be long now.

I said "In a little while you may see some familiar faces. If anyone joins us at the table, you go hang out at the bar, Okay? And stay there for a while."

"What about my mozzarella marinara? You've got to eat it hot."

So many problems.

"Tell the waiter. Eat it at the bar."

In about half an hour, Gizzi and Cannizzarro walked into the restaurant together. They stopped to talk with several diners on the way toward our table. There was a ripple of acknowledgement through the room; it was clear the Z's were local celebrities.

Now at our table they greeted us like old acquaintances and slid in next to us in the vast, red vinyl biscuit-tufted banquette. Lou had traded his cardigan for a camel hair cashmere jacket over a white silk shirt, open at the neck, brown whipcord slacks and an enviable pair of Bally slip-on ankle boots. He had his kindly Dean-of-Students look, which might have been more convincing without the collection of gold chains around his neck and the chunky gold and diamond bracelet. Cannizzarro had on his usual sour expression and another Beverly Hills exercise suit. Dark green velour. Easily two hundred fifty dollars at Neiman Marcus. I knew. I had one.

Hersh gave the two hoodlums a look that combined terror and indignation, then got up and went over to the bar.

Cannizzarro said "It's gonna cost nine grand to fix the boat, asshole."

"Tell Larry you can't shift those transmissions over a thousand rpm without blowing them up."

Both of them said "Larry who?"

They looked at each other, than at me. Vic smirked. Lou smiled pleasantly. It didn't look like they intended to smack me around, at least not while we were at Fratianne's. I had a sense that the place was a neutral zone; that the infliction of death or serious bodily injury to a diner at table would get you eighty-sixed for life.

I was having serious doubts. This was another situation I had precipitated without thinking things through, worse than doing the femur fandango. My ability to set up these encounters sometimes turns out to be more reliable than my ability to carry them off. Right then, I couldn't believe I had actually gone looking for these jerks.

"Lets not horse around, fellas," I said. "There's two things you want, and I've got both of them. And I've got something you don't want."

I was babbling; had I really said something that stupid?

"Did you follow that shit?" Vic said to his companion. "And he tells us not to horse around. 'You got it, I want it. I want it, you got it'. Jesus." He shook his head in disgust.

The waiter brought two orders of mozzarella marinara. I took one and told him to take the other to Hersh, at the bar, but Vic grabbed it.

"Let him starve," he said, "the cocksucker."

"Okay," I said, and went into my pitch. "You want Doctor Rayburn and his records. The photographs he took. I've got them. What you don't want is this."

I handed Lou an envelope containing a large color blowup of the Catalina picture. He took it out and looked at it, then passed it to Vic. I ate my deep fried cheese. Cannizzarro's portion was on the table in front of him, getting cold. I think he wanted to take it away from Hersh more than he wanted to eat it.

"It's no good if it gets cold," I said. "the cheese sets up."

Vic said "Huh?" He eyed his plate suspiciously, but started to eat.

As I finished eating, I smelled something burning and looked up. Lou was holding a corner of the Catalina photograph over a candle set in the middle of the table in a red glass holder. The picture was burning brightly. He dropped it into my empty plate, where it fizzled out in the remains of the marinara sauce. None of the other diners seemed to notice. I thought, people must burn things at tables in here all the time. I wondered what would have happened if he had cut my throat.

Vic said "McGuire, you are as fulla shit as a man can get and still be alive." And they slid out of the banquette and left. Hersh came back from the bar and sat down next to me.

He said "What happened to my appetizer?"

*   *   *

I spent another hour at the table with Hersh, working all the way through the menu to espresso in little china cups, and Strega, which tastes better than you think it's going to. Then I put him in a cab, and gave my parking check to the valet sitting outside Fratianne's front door. He gave me a funny look, and I figured out why when he brought me my rented Jeep Cherokee with Larry Hayden sitting in the front passenger seat, in a suit and tie, talking on a cell phone. I paid, and we left, heading west on Little Santa Monica Boulevard.

After a couple of minutes I said "Lou called you when he spotted us in the restaurant, right?"

Larry said "Of course he did. You think I hang around in parking lots?"

"At Fratianne's, maybe."

I had always wanted to drive a Jeep. It handled like a tank, and you could look down on the other drivers. I told Larry about the Catalina picture.

I said "You know what happened at Fratianne's?"

"A little. You should be careful trying to bluff those guys."

"I didn't think it was a bluff," I said, "but I guess they did. They set fire to my ace in the hole."

"That was for drill," he said, "Actually, now that you've explained it, you called it right. They won't want anyone up the chain of command to see the picture you took. It could destroy some long-standing relationships. They're right; I feel the same way."

Larry said "We've got to arrive at an understanding." He drew a deep breath. "For openers, you should know that Mr. Gizzi and his associates are competing with us." Mr. Gizzi. I liked that. "They've got their own system for hiding people."

"What's new?"

"No, I mean a system. New identities, jobs and new faces. That was what Doctor Rayburn was doing for them. That's why we both want the photographs he took in his office."

"Larry, you gave them Doctor Rayburn in Dallas. He told me."

"I didn't say we wanted Rayburn, just the plastic surgery records, and the photographs."

"He trusted you."

"Tom, I've got more than sixty protected witnesses in the Southern California area, more than two hundred people if you count their families. Remember I told you about the guy who wanted to work in a bank, and we couldn't stop him?"

I remembered.

"He embezzled two million dollars. Took it right out of the vault. We were two weeks away from trial. His testimony was crucial. What could we do? He was laughing at us. After he testified, he disappeared with the money."

"The bank ever find out what you folks did to them?"

"Thank God no. But you can't have stuff like that going on. We got him that job with fake documents. Then he turns around and bites our hand. What are we supposed to do? It's like running a big supermarket; you're gonna get rats."

"So you call exterminators?"

"Only once in a while." If he sensed my irony he didn't react to it. "The Witness Protection Program has to appear to work, or nobody would go into it."

"Right. The Roach Motel principle."

"That's not funny. They're not bugs."

"They're not?"

He ignored me "Every so often there'll be a guy we just can't keep, like the embezzler. Somebody who's potentially embarrassing, or a nuisance, a complainer. Your friends back there at Fratianne's take care of it for us."

"You mean Gizzi and Cannizzarro?"

"Yeah."

"They're not my friends, they're your friends."

"Well, whatever. Once in a while I'll give them someone they really want, in exchange for their help. And anyway, we're way over budget. Sometimes you have to thin the herd."

"Like buffalo in Yellowstone Park?"

Silence. We passed Beverly Glen. Larry stared out the window, working up a head of steam. The jeep was handling stiffly, and I was starting to wonder if it was as user-friendly as I thought it was.

Larry said "Cockroaches, buffaloes, you got a hell of an imagination." He paused. "I'm not going to debate morality or ethics with you like we're two kids in college. Everyone involved here has got something to lose, including you and your friends."

I said "Do your superiors at the USA's office know you barter protected witnesses with the forces of evil?"

He shrugged. "You read too many comic books. The Department's getting what it wants; prosecutions of major Mafia figures, big headlines. We're crimefighters. It can be a dirty business."

"I've made two sets of Doctor Rayburn's plastic surgery records," I said. "I'm going to give a set to you and a set to the dickhead twins, okay?"

"Why do you have to do that?"

"I want two things in exchange. Get the guys to lay off Doctor Rayburn, and there's a letter I want you to write to Detective Radovich. Oh, and by the way, I'll throw in the picture I took of you and your troops at Isthmus Cove.

"I don't give a shit what you do with it."

"So I can send one copy to the Attorney General of the

210

United States and one to Harry Hatcher at the *L.A. Times*?"

Larry said "Stop the car." and I pulled over in front of the immense hilly lawn of the Mormon Tabernacle. High atop the storybook building stood the gilded figure of the Angel Moroni, pointing his trumpet toward Salt Lake City.

We sat for a minute, then Larry said "You're playing out of your league." I said nothing. "For the people I have to work with, killing someone is just a business decision."

Which people, I wondered? It didn't matter. I turned to him and put my hand on his shoulder.

I said "It's your game. They'll kill you before they kill me."

A generic all-purpose threat. He looked intimidated, so I assumed it must have meant something to him.

*　　*　　*

Thinking back on it, what strikes me is how little I reacted to the corrupt mess Larry had made of his job. When I was little there was a time when I got into fights at school, PS 162, so my father put me in a Catholic school. Stop fighting, his message was, and you can go back to public school. At the same time, my mother was insisting on Hebrew school three times a week after regular school. The Irish-Jewish tortures of my childhood. Inevitably, the Sisters found out about the Rabbis, and vice versa. I couldn't believe I had managed to make so many people so mad at me. When it came time to go to seventh grade I walked into the local junior high school and registered myself. At that point, and forever afterwards, I refused to go anywhere near the Sisters or the Rabbis. The experience left me with a certain detachment. I would visualize everyone's beliefs hovering over the Earth in a big black ball, like a bomb, waiting to fall on my head. I think that big black ball has been up there ever since. It takes a lot of effort to keep it from falling.

*　　*　　*

211

Back at the boat Maria was asleep. She woke up when I came aboard and I filled her in on my evening.

She said "Did you get what you wanted?"

"Yeah. I guess. Nobody cares about the Doctor anymore, now that they're going to get his files. I never realized what Larry was up to, with the witnesses."

"You mean the roach motel business?"

"Yeah, that, but trading them to the other side like baseball players?"

She made a face. "Who knows about it?"

"I do."

She shifted under the covers, exposing one breast and reminding me that, as always, she slept naked.

She said "They're going to leave your friend alone?"

"Murray?"

"Yes."

"Nobody ever wanted Murray. They wanted Doctor Rayburn and Murray was taking care of him."

"And you're going to give his plastic surgery files to the Government?"

"Not exactly. I'm going to give Larry copies."

"He's not the Government?"

I said "You mean is he going to turn those files over to his bosses? No, I don't expect he will."

She turned over in bed so she was facing away from me. Not a promising development.

I said "After all this, I'm not sure who's side I'm on."

"Do you have to be on a side? Anyway, why ask that question now? Isn't the game over?"

I had shucked off my clothes. I said "Move over." I got in bed and curled against her back, making the stacked spoons.

"Tom," she said, "you are a child."

Right then I didn't feel like a child at all.

34

When a warm wind blows steadily across Los Angeles it's called a Santa Ana condition. It blows smog off the sides of the mountains that ring the Los Angeles Basin and takes it out to sea, where it reappears as a bourbon-colored band on the horizon. Prevailing ocean swells in Santa Monica Bay are from the Northwest, and a Santa Ana condition tends to flatten them out, producing calm water and clear warm days.

These are excellent conditions for boating and fishing. That's what Maria and I were doing; boating and fishing, and canoodling. We were six or eight miles off Marina del Rey, soaking a mackerel for shark and being naughty. The location provides complete privacy. As long as you keep an eye out for silent-running sailboats, you might as well be on the moon. On the minus side there are space limitations presented by a sixteen foot open powerboat, and the possibility of sunburn on areas usually covered by a bathing suit.

Drifting for shark is a low-key operation, until you hook up. The way it works is, you drift a dead mackerel on wire leader and set the clicker on the reel so you can hear if line is being pulled out. After that you don't have to pay attention until a shark grabs your mackerel and starts swimming away with it, pulling out line and making the clicker buzz. Then you pick up your fishing pole, tighten the drag, pull back with the rod a couple of times to set the hook, and you've got a shark on. In Santa Monica Bay it could be a blue shark, Mako, Thresher very rarely, or Hammerhead almost never. The Makos are the ones that jump and dance on their tails. Most sharks just hunker down and tug. You tug back. A lot of fishermen go out with heavy tackle and basically yank their sharks out of the water. Even with light tackle if you know what you're doing it's really not much of a contest. Gill-netters have seriously reduced the shark population off Southern California, and Maria and I hardly ever keep our catch. I don't enjoy it as much as I used to when I did it all the time and my friends started calling me Sharky.

Everyone has two reasons for everything they do; a good reason and the real reason. If you come back to the Marina with a shark on your transom people will think you've got balls that clank. That's the reason a lot of people do it. On the other hand, for Maria and me there's the sex. It can lead to some comical situations. If you do get a hookup there's no time to waste, and I have found myself fighting a shark while undressed. It's a matter of timing, Maria's and mine, and the shark's.

"It's like Groucho Marx's line about shooting an elephant in his pajamas."

Maria said "What are you talking about?"

"The Marx Brothers."

"I told you you should reel in your mackerel if you were feeling lovey."

Trying to do two things at once.

"You know," I said, "Kate Balducci's out here."

"Her ashes, you mean."

"Yeah. And whoever they got to take Doctor Rayburn's place. They threw his ashes in the Bay too."

We drifted on the flat water, in the warm glare. The last shark had stolen the bait and I was feeling too relaxed to put another mackerel on. Maria was beautiful in the sunshine, free of her little yellow bikini and now wearing only her straw hat and sunglasses.

She said "What do you want done with your remains when you're gone?"

"Why? Do you know something I don't?"

"Just asking. My family has a plot in San Gabriel. There's room for me there."

I considered it for a moment.

"It's a cheerful thought," I said. "I won't be joining you, though. I want my remains to be scattered from an airplane."

"Oh?"

"Yeah. Without cremation. Over Beverly Hills on trash morning."

She smiled a little.

"You make a joke out of everything to keep reality from getting too close."

"You're absolutely right," I said. "I've made a career out of it."

"Tom, are we still in trouble?"

"Well, Lee Brown says they're going to have to dismiss the case against us."

"That's nice. It means I can keep my job." She stood up and started applying sunblock to her thighs.

I said "Everybody got what they wanted; the Government, the goons. I don't have anything anyone needs any more."

She patted me lovingly in a way she could only have done in private.

"I wouldn't say that," she said.

Some time passed. We drifted in silence. There were ham sandwiches from the Normandie, and we ate them. There was a nice Beaujolais varietal, a Fleurie.

Maria said "What happened to Doctor Rayburn?"

"Larry told me Rayburn was going to have to stay dead, to avoid any embarrassment to the Department of Justice."

"That's what he said?"

"Yeah."

"So where did they put him?"

"Murray can't find him, so I imagine he's back being a protected witness again. In any case, he won't be making any court appearances to testify for the Government. They don't allow dead people to testify."

"No, I suppose not. But they always knew that would be a problem, didn't they?"

"Larry was working the deep end of the pool. Don't forget, this is a guy who spent most of his professional lifetime prosecuting people for interstate auto theft, things like that. He didn't have a lot of training in witness protection. I think he just made mistakes."

"So it was a learning process."

"Right. So was Custer's Last Stand. In my opinion Larry's next big problem may be the dead sailor they came up with at the Veterans Administration Hospital. He belonged to somebody. I doubt anybody's prepared to take responsibility for stealing him."

Maria said "Our Government shouldn't be stealing corpses."

"That's it," I said, "it would be wrong."

I put a mackerel out and we drifted. There was a false alarm involving a harbor seal. I put another mackerel out.

Maria said "Did you know that there's gold in seawater?"

"No," I said. "Can you get it out?"

"That's what the article I read was about. There's pounds of gold in every cubic mile of seawater, or something like that. So all you would have to do is get a boat and drive it around with a pump, and some kind of a machine that would separate out the gold as it went through the pipe, and you could have all the gold you wanted."

217

"Yeah," I said, "but is there such a machine?"

She gazed over the side. This far offshore the water was an astonishing deep blue. Inshore it looked like shit, for a very good reason.

She said "No, I don't think anyone's perfected it. But people are trying."

It reminded me of Hersh, and the plan I had discussed with him at Fratianni's.

I said "That's just the kind of thing Hersh would have used in the old days when he did shell promotions."

She looked puzzled, so I explained it to her. When Hersh was Horace Templeton, and occupied a place of prominence on the Justice Department's Securities Violator list, he would take over a defunct publicly-held corporation, a 'public shell' as they're called, and find somebody to put up some money and be its new president. Maybe a wealthy doctor with time on his hands. One of Hersh's stooges would offer the company an incredible opportunity to help develop a machine that extracted gold from seawater, say. Publicity would be prepared and disseminated into the marketplace, brokers would be bribed to open a public market and recommend the stock to greedy and stupid investors, then Hersh would sell his huge position in the stock into the market little by little until it could absorb no more. The market would tank. Hersh would go away. People would get mad.

Maria said "That's it? Wouldn't the Government catch up with him?"

"In those days the thing about white collar crime was they let you keep the money. A couple of times Hersh had to sign Consent Decrees with the SEC. That's a promise not to do it again. They wouldn't ask him to give back what he had stolen from the public investors. They've changed all that these days. Now if you do what Hersh used to do you get indicted and put in prison. Takes the fun out of it."

"I never realized Hersh was such a crook," she said. "He seems so harmless."

"That's one of his great talents. They call them

confidence men because they inspire confidence. Actually, it's a kind of genius. After I left the Government he came to my office and tried to get me to do the legal work for one of his public deals. For stock. But the stock was going to be worth millions. The story had to be bullshit. I knew that if I decided to work for him I'd have the SEC all over me inside of six months. And I still believed he was going to make me rich. It was eerie. There's some kind of force involved. I think it's hypnotism. I had to keep repeating to myself 'Tom, remember who this guy is. He's fulla shit.' And even then I couldn't get it out of my head; 'I'm going to be rich. I'll be able to close my office and take it easy.' It was a strange experience."

"It was greed, Tom. It's like flattery. Even when you think you know it's happening, it can still work on you."

"I suppose. I came back to my office the next day and called him, told him I couldn't do it. But in a way I admired the man. It takes a special talent to inspire other people to believe in something you know isn't true."

"It's not talent," Maria said, "it's a sociopathic personality."

"Sometimes people like that can be useful."

35

There was a message on the machine from Tootie Tenuta when we got back to the boat. He was there to answer the phone when I called him back. I like that in a person.

"Tom! My lighthouse in the storm."

"Really Tootie, you don't have to say that"

"You'll never know. If it wasn't for you I'd be taking one in the slats right now from Bubba."

It was a new perspective.

"Okay, listen," he went on, "you wanted to know about me finding things, so I figured I'd tell you. Howard and I talked about it and I said it was embarrassing. I told him about being called Ray Charles on accounta he's blind, right? And they kid me that I never find anything on the job?"

"I remember."

"Okay, so Howard likes me, you know what I mean? Because I'm married to Ruthie, his sister?"

"Right. Ruthie."

"Maybe she said something to him. I don't know. But next Monday Howard says I can find things, some good stuff. So I can hold my head up with the boys, the other Monitors, and not feel like a schmuck."

"Where Monday?"

"Up in Topanga. We're starting a new job on Stunt Road, a big lot for a house. For a movie star, I don't know who. Howard says there's gonna be a lotta action there."

"What kind of action?"

"Native American stuff. Graves, probably. The real thing. The kinda things we'll find, Howard says they'll put it in the papers. Maybe even come up and take pictures. I'll feel better about the gig if I can find stuff. I'm tired of this Ray Charles business."

Just like Vic Cannizzarro. Everyone needs sulfa steam.

"Tootie, how does Howard know in advance there'll be things for you to find next Monday?"

Tootie was silent for a moment.

"Tom..." He hesitated. "...maybe you don't wanna ask me that. Before Howard made me into an Indian I was just some dickhead driving a cab. I thought you'd be proud of me, that's all."

"I am proud, Tootie. Forget I asked. Can I come see you in action?"

He gave me directions. "Come early, before Howard gets there. We start at eight."

"I'll bring coffee and doughnuts."

"Nah. We got a cooler full of Tecate."

"Breakfast of champions."

"No shit, Tom. See ya Monday."

Down below, Maria was putting away groceries I had just brought aboard with the dock cart.

I said "Do you want to go on a picnic?"

"Where?"

"Topanga. Way up near the top."

That got her attention. "I haven't been up there in years," she said. "We've never been up there together, except..."

"On the Harley. I was riding bitch."

"Tom, do you honestly think it's effeminate to ride on the back of a motorcycle?"

It was a difficult call. I didn't actually think so, but when I'm in back and Maria is driving I've seen some people look amused.

"I've seen some people look amused, that's all. I'm riding bitch and there's a woman in front."

Maria said "Those people are bikers who are insecure about their masculinity."

"Good thing I don't have that problem."

*   *   *

We had no trouble finding the site Tootie had told me about. There were surveyor's stakes with little fluttering red rags tied to the tops. A small amount of earth had been disturbed right at the edge of the road. and some temporary-looking electric lines led down to a junction box. A large wooden sign said 'Westside Construction' with an address and telephone number. The site was high up in Topanga at the top of Stunt Road. It had a panoramic view of the San Fernando Valley.

Maria said "You'd think for a movie star the place would be on the other side, looking down on the Bay."

"Maybe the guy's in television."

It was really a beautiful piece of land, gently sloping down toward the northeast from the frontage, with a small hill rising back up on one side, and rocky outcroppings at the back, ending in a dropoff, a natural barrier between the parcel and the downslope neighbor, if there was one. It was overgrown with scrub pine and eucalyptus, with what looked like sage and greasewood or creosote growing beneath the trees. It looked tough; not conducive to a picnic. Soon, I thought, it would be stripped bare by the bulldozers of Westside Construction.

We went on a hundred yards or so down the road, left the bike at a turnout, and walked back with our lunch. We had an olive bread from Il Forniao, a substantial hunk of Morbier cheese and some smoked chicken breast. And a white Bordeaux. Maria didn't believe in going very far from home without a bottle of white Bordeaux.

Maria sat at the top of the rocky outcrop at the back of the property and set out the food on a little cloth while I walked around. It was a large parcel for a residence, maybe five acres, with most of it useable as long as you were willing to tear out all the vegetation. What the hell, you could buy trees later. This is L.A.; trees you want, trees you got. I found a number of filled-in holes and trenches which I knew were the results of the subsoil investigation that had been necessary to get a building permit. I spent some time poking around, then returned to our makeshift picnic table.

Forty-five minutes later we had finished lunch and were getting ready to leave when up the slope at the road frontage an unmarked panel truck slowed and stopped. Two men got out, walked to the back and opened the rear cargo doors. They were the two beefy car-batterers from Century City.

"Uh-oh," I said. "Heckel and Jeckel."

"Who?"

"Trouble. Those guys probably know my face. Let's go."

We gathered up our gear, scrambled down behind the rocky ledge and were out of sight of the road. Then we contoured along the hillside through thick brush in the direction of the Harley until we were far enough away to look for a way back uphill. The nice glow induced by the Bordeaux was ruined. We were overheated, and scratched by the brush. The Harley was as we had left it.

Maria said "Those were the guys who banged up your car?"

"Yeah. They've probably got their baseball bats in the van. They're Yonkers Chumash."

"They're what?"

"Phony Indians. Muscle for Howard Running Bear."

"What are they doing here on Saturday? I thought Tootie said it was going to start on Monday?"

"I think I know," I said. "I'll tell you later."

We stowed the remains of lunch in one of Maria's saddlebags and walked the bike most of the way back toward the building site until we could see the area marked by surveyor's stakes, and the van. Frick and Frack were not in sight, and then they appeared, working their way up the hill toward the road, through the thick brush. Each had a burlap sack and a shovel. Right then Murphy's Law kicked in; one of them called out to the other, and pointed toward us. They both stood and stared in our direction.

I said "Oh shit."

Maria said "Wanna see a trick?" and she straddled the Harley, kick-started it and took off toward the van. I drew back into the trees. The two figures stood with their sacks and shovels, then started up toward the road. She definitely had their attention. I was too far away to hear their voices, but if you've ever seen a silent movie you know how much meaning can be packed into gesture and body language. The figure of Maria seemed to say 'So, what are you boys up to on this fine Saturday in Topanga?' The two figures holding shovels seemed to say 'Just having a good time, and taking care of some business. Nothing much.' She gestured down the hill and seemed to say 'Something something, they're going to build here?' They made 'who knows' gestures. Then they exchanged looks and both moved too close to Maria, who was still sitting on the Harley. They seemed to say 'You're awful cute to be out here all by yourself.' One of them put his hand on a handlebar while the other moved back out of Maria's angle of vision. She reached down, then dismounted. Her back was toward me. The scene froze for a moment, then the two men started to move slowly away, walking backwards. They both seemed to be saying 'what is this, now? No need to get upset.' Then Maria got back on the bike, wheeled around and came back toward me. When she was out of sight of the van she stopped long enough for me to jump on the back, and we took off down Stunt Road.

I said "What were those guys doing?"

"Before I showed up? They were digging. They had

224

shovels. But I think they wanted to get me in their van."

"How'd you back them off?"

"Easy. I offered to shoot them."

She reached into a leather pouch by the gas tank and pulled out the .357 Smith & Wesson with the five-inch barrel. Then she put it back.

Maria said "I explained to them about Glaser rounds, but I think they already knew."

Maria had explained to me that Glaser rounds were 'safe' ammunition because they acted as super hollow-points; they expanded enormously when striking flesh, and consequently wouldn't travel through your target and go on to hit someone you didn't even know a half-mile away. You had to learn to think like a handgun enthusiast; the bullets could turn someone into ground round in an instant, but they were 'safe' because after they did that, they stopped.

I said "It's a reversal of traditional gender-determined roles"

Maria said "What is?"

"I'm riding bitch and you're shooting hollow-points."

"I didn't shoot anybody, did I?"

36

Murray and Hersh sat opposite me in *Den Mother's* salon. I had asked them to dress like successful real estate developers and they had done a great job. Hersh was wearing a just-pressed charcoal gray wool suit with a faint chalk stripe, an English club tie, discreet gold cufflinks and a pair of old but brilliantly polished pebble grain cordovan wing-tips. His hair had long been completely gray, but was carefully barbered, and he had tuned up the intense sincere gaze that had made possible a long successful career in securities fraud. I would believe this guy, I thought, if he told me the sky was green. Murray Markoff made a perfect foil to Hersh's Bank-of-England presence; his deep tan was nicely set off by a dove-gray summer-weight flannel suit, light blue shirt and white filigree tie. He grinned at me, looking puckish; an eccentric rich guy. Without the fancy duds he was a retired bookie, or worse, an aging beach bum. With the suit he looked like Bernie Cornfeld; rich and zany. It's an old story; give a poor lunatic money and you get an eccentric millionaire. It's bullshit, but bullshit makes the world go round.

This well-turned-out duo had had years of practice together mismanaging the Southern California Sea Pioneers. They had solicited donations, paid and collected bribes, misappropriated funds, bought and sold boats. Together, they were a walking dog-and-pony show. Howard Running Bear hadn't had a chance.

"You two are beautiful," I said. "I'm glad you gave me a chance to see you in full battle gear. Anybody would believe you were real estate developers."

Murray grinned. Hersh looked vaguely hurt. It's a funny thing about Hersh; he really got into his roles. It was as if I had offended him to suggest that he was not what he and Murray had gone into Howard Running Bear's office pretending that they were. Like a little kid who puts on a cape and says 'I'm Superman,' then pouts when an adult says 'no you're not.'

Hersh said "Howard's not as smart as he thinks he is. And I think he's got cash flow problems. All I had to do was tell him I wanted to pay him some money. After that it was easy."

I said "So you just flat out said you wanted him to put bones on someone else's property to screw up a development?"

Hersh looked pained.

"My dear boy, it is never necessary to be so crude. You can scare people doing that. We told him we wanted an archaeological survey on the Sea Pioneers' parcel before we went ahead with a subdivision. Standard stuff for him. He gave us a price for it, so much per acre. Once we got him started I explained how our development plans would be ruined if Carruthers went ahead with his proposal to build fifty homes up the road. It took him about two minutes to figure out that we wanted him to plant things on Carruthers' property."

"Yeah," Murray said. "And when he got the idea it was

227

a scam on Carruthers, right away the price goes up. Checking out our place was going to be two grand; putting the kibosh on Carruthers was seven and a half."

"Seventy-five hundred?" I had hoped the sting could be brought off without actually paying anything since nobody had offered to bankroll my efforts. "You didn't pay it, did you?"

"Yes," said Hersh. "With a bad check." He smiled a reassuring smile. "I told him I couldn't get the Pioneers involved directly, but I was going to wash money through my mother's account in New Jersey."

"Your mother would have to be at least a hundred years old," I said.

"My mother is long gone these many years," Hersh said, "but I've kept her checking account open. You never know when you're going to need a bank account that's far away. People assume that checks will take longer to clear. It gives you wiggle room."

I said "And Howard bought it, the mother business?"

Hersh smiled. "It's funny. When you say you're going to wash money through your old mother's account it should sound fishy, but actually it's the other way around. People think it must be legitimate or you wouldn't involve your mother. And her name and address is right there on the check, so you figure you'll always be able to find her. Who would get his mother involved in a scam?"

Murray said "Tell him about the check. That's the beauty part."

Hersh made a modest 'aw shucks' gesture. "What you do is alter the micro-encoding at the bottom of the check, just take a pen and screw it up a little. When the bank runs it through the automatic equipment it gets spit out because the machine can't read it. The check goes into a reject pile and an actual human being has to route it by hand. Then, when it gets where it's going the machines at that bank can't read it either. They don't think it's their check, so they send it back to the bank where it was deposited, and nobody knows it's NSF yet. It can go back and forth two or three times, if you get lucky. I found out after Mother died that with this particular bank, for some reason, it could take more than ninety days for the check to finally come back for insufficient funds. Well, at my worst if I couldn't get a deal done inside of ninety days I'd say hang it up and get a job."

"So," I said, "Howard is still waiting for the check to clear?"

Hersh said "Better than that. He probably got credit for the check when he deposited it, so he's spent the money. As far as he knows he's been paid. It's a done deal. Sooner or later his bank will charge it back and he'll have a seventy-five hundred dollar debit."

Murray said "On him it looks good. Fuckin' Tonto with an attitude."

Howard had introduced Hersh and Murray to the people who were actually going to do the work. He described them as "field archaeologists," but the descriptions matched the two weightlifter-types I had encountered in Century City and in Topanga, up on Stunt Road. It turned out they were known as the Badger Brothers. No surprise there.

Then we watched the videotape.

"What we did," Murray explained, "was to hang out in the trailer for a few days. You can't see the trailer from the road, but you can check out the cars coming up the hill. Nobody comes up there by accident. The first weekend after we paid the jerk his seven-and-a-half large, on Saturday late afternoon, comes the two *shtarkers* in a nice big Lincoln." Another Lincoln, to replace the one I burned. "After they passed the trailer on the way up, we followed them. The rest was easy."

It had taken the Badger Brothers more than an hour, which made for a boring videotape. You could see Carruthers' house on the tape, the ridge of the San Gabriel Mountains behind it to the South, and the Lincoln, plainly enough to make out the license plate. Howard Running Bear's meaty assistants were also plainly visible, as they dug holes in Carruthers' stony soil and buried things they brought from the car. You couldn't tell what they were

229

burying, but Hersh had thought of that. The last segment of videotape showed Murray digging some of it up, complete with close-up views of the uncovered objects; human bones, by now a familiar sight to me.

Hersh said "We left some of it where they buried it, but we marked the spots. Anyway it was far too hot to dig."

"Not too hot for me to dig, boss," said Murray.

Hersh affected not to hear. "This is what we collected," he said, gesturing to a large cardboard box they had brought with them.

I opened the box and examined its contents.

"Boys," I said, "these bones will rise again."

37

The week before, my car had been declared a total loss by a suspicious insurance adjuster. The police report had characterized the violent events at Red South Twelve as malicious mischief. The adjuster was dubious.

"Do you have any enemies?" he said.

I said "How long have you been an insurance adjuster?"

"What's that got to do with it?"

"Do you have any enemies?"

"Excuse me, counselor -"

"-Whenever someone like you calls a lawyer 'counselor' he really means to say 'asshole.'"

I could hear him sigh at the other end of the phone. I

hadn't paid anything for the car in the first place. Why struggle?

"Actually," I said, "I'm being harassed by an Indian tribe."

I expected this statement to unleash a flurry of questions but to my surprise it didn't, and he got off the phone quickly after that.

When I called the place that had rented me the Jeep Cherokee I learned I could rent a limousine and driver for a hundred dollars more per day. I thought a limo would be perfect to go see Tootie Tenuta make his bones as a Native American Construction Monitor. The driver would come down to the Marina and pick us up early Monday morning.

So now that I had a tank, I thought I'd raise an army to put inside. In addition to Maria, I mean. I thought of Bruce, the sculptor with the shotgun, but when I called him he reminded me that he was on probation and had been ordered to get rid of the shotgun and not to possess any firearms. So Bruce was out. Moe the weightlifter and sometimes counterfeiter told me he was scheduled to participate in a bodybuilding competition, Mr. Venice Beach, in a week. He called it a 'pose-down.' He said he couldn't do anything that might get him bruised, but he agreed to come along. I thought his presence would discourage hostilities. I hoped for a peaceful morning in Topanga, but I had done my best to stir up as much trouble as possible, and it doesn't hurt to anticipate the worst.

I had the limo driver pick up Moe first, then stop at the Marina for Maria and me. The driver was a Turk. Yasman, he said. A short, intense, dark-skinned man in a white shirt, black pants, black bow tie and vaguely military khaki jacket. He had deep, troubled dark eyes. He chain-smoked unfiltered Camels in the front seat behind the pane of glass that separated him from his passengers.

*   *   *

Stunt Road was quiet at eight o'clock on a Monday

morning. It was cool and sunny. At the building site Westside Construction had installed a construction shack, and a portable outhouse. A few pieces of bright yellow grading equipment were parked at the side of the road. Nothing seemed to be happening. I thought I recognized the van that the Badger Brothers had used on Saturday when Maria and I had our picnic. I told Yasman to keep going, and made some calls from my cell phone. There was a TV and a bar. It was a nice limo. I felt I had done the right thing.

When we returned it was eleven-thirty. Things were developing nicely. One bulldozer was at work scraping up vegetation and dumping it in a pile at the side of the road. A cluster of people stood watching the work being done. I recognized Tootie in a blue and white plaid shirt and long black ponytail. He had a can of beer in his hand. I figured that Howard Running Bear would have planned the first discoveries for about ten-thirty or eleven, so he could call the media for a show at the construction site by two or three that afternoon; in time to make the evening news. I wasn't sure how much Howard knew about public relations, so I had helped out a little.

I had spoken to Harry Hatcher of the *L.A. Times* on Sunday, and filled him in. I had done the same with the City News Service, to make sure that all the TV stations and anyone else who cared would hear about the big jamboree that was going to happen on Stunt Road.

We parked about a hundred yards past the site and waited. Yasman got out of the limo and lit another Camel, polished the left front fender with a cloth and then leaned against it as he smoked. I thought I heard a helicopter. A couple of big old sedans drove up and parked close to the construction trailer, and six or eight middle-aged men got out. They had strong faces that made me think of Iron Eyes Cody, the one who made you cry in the TV commercial. Maria said they were Indians. I certainly hoped so, since I had spent two hours the day before calling every tribal representative in Southern California, from a long list helpfully provided by the California Native American Heritage

Commission. The ones I had gotten through to had been very surprised to hear from me.

If you had seen one or two of these men walking on a city street you might have thought they looked different from your average citizen, without realizing why that was so. It wasn't the occasional piece of western wear, the leather fringe, pointy boots, or this or that silver or turquoise ornament or belt buckle. It wasn't the hair, black and worn long or in a braid. These men had not dressed up for a celebration, not after what I had told them was going to happen at the Stunt Road jobsite.

It was the eyes. Their eyes seemed to look out from a place I had never been and to see a world that I would never know. More than any other culture, history had chewed these people up and spit them out. These men knew this, with their worn plaid shirts and thousand-yard stares; knew that it had once been their world, and that what had happened to it could never be made right. Streets and buildings now stood where the forbearers of these men lived lives that are now understood to have reflected the Nineteenth Century romantic ideal of the Noble Savage. What irony. Even their memories have been stolen, and replaced with gushy evocations of a world that never was. That, and Hollywood movies of the forties and fifties in which painted warriors attacked settlers' wagon trains. Which I understand actually happened from time to time.

I'd be pissed off too, particularly if someone told me that imposters in Malibu were running a scam with my history and relics of my past. Judging from the expressions on the faces of the Indians who were arriving at Stunt Road, my expectations for the morning had been too conservative. I had figured the Malibu Band of the Chumash Nation might not survive; now I had my doubts about Howard Running Bear. Too late now.

More cars arrived. More Indians got out. I watched with binoculars. An enormous black Lincoln Navigator SUV appeared, bearing a pair of longhorn steer horns as a hood ornament. You can sometimes see these wicked-looking things on the hoods of pickup trucks in places like Montana. Howard Running Bear emerged from the SUV and entered the construction shack. A few minutes later one of the Badger Brothers was observed walking purposefully in our direction. No baseball bat; this time he carried a shovel. As he closed on us I got out to meet him, telling Maria to stay inside the limo. Moe appeared to be asleep.

"Mr. Running Bear says get lost," he said. "You've got no business here." He carried his shovel over his shoulder like a rifle.

I could see Moe stirring in the backseat of the limo. Then he got out and stood staring at the heavily muscled man with the shovel.

"Arnie?" he said.

Yasman flicked away his cigarette and turned to watch.

"Arnie, what're you doing up here?"

Howard Running Bear's henchman looked at Moe, then over his shoulder toward the construction shack, then shifted his shovel to the port arms position.

"Shut up." he said.

Moe turned to me. "That's Arnie Logan. He works out with me at World Gym. He's going to do the pose-down with me next week. Mr. Venice Beach."

Arnie said "Shut up, Moe," then turned toward me, shifting the shovel from port arms to his shoulder again.

He said "You burned up my car, you motherfucker."

He raised the shovel from his shoulder with both hands and took a step toward the limo, like a batter stepping into a low outside pitch. Yasman darted out from the other side of the limo and punched him in the crotch. A short hard jab. Moe laughed. Arnie dropped the shovel and fell to the ground, clasping his crotch with both hands. Maria got out of the limo to watch.

Yasman looked at me apologetically and said "It is my limousine, you see. I am the owner, not merely a servant. Too many assholes like this man are making damage. I am sorry." He adjusted his bow tie. "You wish to remain here?"

I said that I did.

Yasman got a roll of duct tape out of the trunk and approached the fallen Arnie. "Please, sir, remain as you are," he said, and started wrapping Arnie's ankles with tape. Arnie was busy with his balls, but managed to kick his feet against the duct tape. Then Maria took the Magnum out of her purse and pointed it at his head, and he was still. Yasman pulled Arnie's hands away from his crotch and taped them behind his back.

"It is excellent, this tape," he said as he worked, "very useful for many things," adding a final piece over Arnie's mouth.

I said "You seem to know what you're doing."

"In my country I was a policeman."

Arnie lay where he had fallen. It didn't look like anyone had seen the confrontation. Moe and I dragged him around to the far side of the limo and placed him carefully in a shallow ditch that ran alongside the road.

Nothing happened for another half-hour, then lots of things started happening at the same time. Two TV remote vans appeared and set up. Harry Hatcher arrived in another van, with two photographers. Soon there was a small crowd of people wandering around, some with minicams or other communications equipment on their shoulders. Everyone was talking into cell phones. The TV cameras set up in front of the construction shack, where there was a porch with a railing in front of the door. It made a kind of podium and looked like the location of the coming media event. A guy driving a lunchwagon on his way to somewhere else saw a better opportunity, pulled over and opened for business. A kind of light carnival atmosphere began to develop. I noticed a few uniformed policemen. There were two or three helicopters buzzing around overhead. It was time to get out there and circulate.

The three of us left the limo with Yasman and walked down to the action. Nobody paid any attention to us. People were wandering all over the construction site, no doubt looking for archaeological treasures, or at least I damn well

237

hoped they were, since I had salted the area with my entire collection of bones the day before. Between the bones *Senor* Salas had brought me and the ones Murray had dug up on Carruthers' property I had quite a large supply. I had put some of the larger bones up in trees, to make sure they wouldn't be missed. They were not being missed. The Indians, in particular, were spending a lot of time looking. The more they looked, and found, it seemed the madder they got. Most of the Indians I had spoken to on the phone hadn't believed what I told them. It was different now. Indians were talking to reporters and cameramen here and there. An edgy mood started to develop.

Someone was pounding on the door to the construction shack, and shouting for Howard. Police converged on the disturbance, which attracted the crowd's attention.

Now, people were throwing stones at the construction shack, breaking its windows. Finally, someone forced the door and the crowd surged forward. Three uniformed policemen tried to prevent people from entering. At this point it became a riot. Helicopters came down low to get dramatic pictures. This added lots of noise to the scene and made it more exciting than it already was. Finally the construction shack was torn apart. So was the outhouse next door. Things were getting wild and I thought it would be a good time to leave.

We returned to the limo. Yasman had dragged a few fallen branches over Arnie so he wouldn't be seen from the air. I thought about removing the branches and, maybe, pulling the tape off Arnie's ankles just before we left. On further reflection I decided to leave him as he was. Someone would discover him before too long, and if not, he could deal with the coyotes.

On the way home we turned on the TV in the limo and watched the story on the four o'clock news. There was a lot of confusing videotape and various suggestions as to what it meant, but nobody had the big picture.

By evening the TV news shows had it all sorted out.

Southern California's population of Native Americans had been demonstrating against the desecration of their ancestors' graves. Native American human remains had been used in an attempt to frustrate development of a lot on Stunt Road. Most of the bones found on the jobsite had museum markings indicating they came from the collection of the Museum of the West. Channel Two had taped an interview with Morris Bissette, Curator of Native American Artifacts at the Museum of the West. He explained why the bones weren't the Museum's property any more and what had probably happened to them after they were turned over to a representative of the Malibu Chumash, who he identified as 'Mr. Bear.' Howard Running Bear had been severely beaten during the riot. He was found impaled on the longhorn hood ornament of his SUV, and was now in intensive care. One of the more photogenic of the Tribal leaders was given a minute on screen to explain to a sympathetic anchor person about the desecration of his ancestors' graves. There was lots of helicopter footage of people running around, destroying property, getting arrested, and so on. I could see our limo, but not Arnie.

Harry Hatcher's piece would come out the next morning in the *L.A. Times* I had pointed out to him the possibilities of interviews with Hersh, who had videotape of Howard Running Bear's 'field archaeologists' actually doing what everyone now knew they tried to do on Stunt Road, and with Franco Mandelbrot, who would be happy to explain what it meant to discover a trove of ancient bones on a development site in Los Angeles County. And Detective Radovich, who I thought could use his fifteen minutes of fame, to tell about the murder of the Environmental Lady, found at another development site with the same kind of bones with the same inked-on markings as were found on Stunt Road. The widowed Victor Balducci would probably like a chance to explain about Kate, and her crusade against development in Malibu, or maybe not. It was his call. And then there was the Malibu City Archaeologist, and the Cultural Heritage Officer, and maybe whoever owned

239

Museum Pieces, who might want an opportunity to explain why it was legal for that company to resell ancient human remains it got from Howard Running Bear. The possibilities were many, and I tried to keep ahead of things by calling media people and making suggestions. I have always been a helpful kind of person, and every once in a while it's satisfying to see the bad guys take one in the shorts.

Within three days there was a fire in Century City at the offices of the Malibu Band of the Chumash Nation. If coyotes had eaten the duct-taped body of Arnie, the Badger Brother, it did not make the newspapers. Nobody had seen any of Howard Running Bear's followers. I assumed they would all go back to being whatever they had been before an obliging Registrar in Yonkers New York had made them Chumash Indians. That was the one thing I held back. My plans had worked out well enough without taking Tootie Tenuta down and ruining his future as a Native American Construction Monitor. He would never keep the job if they found out he was an Italian-American cabdriver with a felony sheet. Tootie was a nice guy, and I thought he looked good in his new persona as an Indian, complete with ponytail and can of Tecate, the favorite beer of the Cultural Heritage set.

38

Hersh made serious money selling the Carruthers tape to the TV news show 'Hard Copy.' Murray was on the phone telling me this, pissed off that Hersh wouldn't give him any of the money.

"He makes thousands, the cheap son of a bitch, and to me he gives *bupkis*."

I said "What are you complaining about? It was my idea to make the tape in the first place. He didn't give me anything either."

"Yeah, maybe so, but, dammit, that's me digging up those bones. It was hot. I worked hard. I'm an old man. Everybody I know tells me they've seen it on TV, and then they say, 'I'll bet you got some good bread for that,' and like a schmuck I've gotta tell them no, that I got ripped off."

"Lie about it."

"I *do* lie about it. I've got my self respect, but better I should have been paid."

Better we should all have been paid, I thought. We helped the developers, both Mandelbrot and whoever had wanted to build the house on Stunt Road. We helped the Indians. We helped Detective Radovich, who would now be able to get DNA comparisons between Howard Running Bear and the material found beneath Kate Balducci's fingernails after she died. I believed I even helped the Mafia and the Justice Department regain a cooperative working relationship. And how about Doctor Rayburn? I had a recent phone message from him.

When I got Doctor Rayburn on the phone it turned out he was living in the Channel Islands Marina, up in Ventura County, on the sixty-three foot Pacemaker Murray had arranged for him to donate to the Southern California Sea Pioneers. His situation was stranger than I had imagined.

"Now the Government has to protect itself from me," he said.

"Why? Have you threatened them?"

"No, but my existence is a threat. Don't you see, I'm dead, and if you check out the circumstances it makes the Department of Justice look bad. Remember that dead body they got ahold of? That poor man's family would sue in a minute if they found out. And something Larry Hayden said made me think that they played that trick with a corpse more than once."

"Hummh. Cadavergate."

"Right. Actually I think they feel sorry for me. They definitely don't want me telling any part of this story to anyone. I get a little money from them, and I've got a job up here helping to take care of the marina, but I'm a doctor, Tom, I can't practice medicine any more and I'm not used to being poor."

"Yeah. Well, if there's anything I could do to help you out..."

"Actually, I was thinking about my wife."

"You mean your ex?"

"Right. I keep forgetting."

243

"What about her?"

"Well, there's two million dollars of life insurance she collected, and I remember you told me she wouldn't want to hear that I was alive."

"You bet. She'd have to give back the money."

"Exactly. So I was wondering whether if you approached her or her lawyer, if they would agree to split up with me, you know, give me a million to stay dead. She'd still have a lot of money, and then so would I, and I could live a little better. I don't have any money to pay you, but we could share the money if you get any..."

Silence.

"Tom?"

"I'm thinking it over."

About the Author

Jonathan Schwartz was born in Washington DC. After graduating from Bard College and the University of Pennsylvania Law School he went on to work in Washington, DC for the Federal Trade Commission, and, later the Department of Commerce.

He ultimately made the decision to accept an SEC position in Los Angeles, and decided to make Southern California his home.

He now lives and practices law in Marina del Rey, California, where his private law practice is limited exclusively to securities regulation, disputes between broker-dealers and customers, securities fraud, and enforcement.

He worked his way through college as a professional musician and has performed stand-up comedy at numerous venues in the Los Angeles area.

All three novels featuring Attorney Tom McGuire are now available through Amazon.com at **www.legalmystery.com**

www.ingramcontent.com/pod-product-compliance
Lightning Source LLC
Chambersburg PA
CBHW071834020726
47502CB00004B/1352